CAPITAL OBSESSION

MAPLE SYRUP MYSTERIES

EMILY JAMES

STRONGHOLD BOOKS

Emily James

authoremilyjames@gmail.com

www.authoremilyjames.com

This is a work of fiction. I made it up. You are not in my book. I probably don't even know you. If you're confused about the difference between real life and fiction, you might want to call a counselor rather than a lawyer because names, characters, places, and incidents in this book are a product of my twisted imagination. Real locales and public names are sometimes used for atmospheric purposes. Any resemblance to actual people, living or dead, or to businesses, companies, events, and institutions is completely coincidental.

Editor: Christopher Saylor at
www.saylorediting.wordpress.com/services/

Cover Design: Deranged Doctor Design at
www.derangeddoctordesign.com

Published August 2017 by Stronghold Books

ISBN: 978-1-988480-10-7

ALSO BY EMILY JAMES

Maple Syrup Mysteries

To all the people who told me I was crazy for wanting to be an author. Thank you. You made me more determined than I otherwise might have been to make my dream come true.

And to anyone who has ever been told their dream is crazy. Crazy doesn't mean impossible.

The most dangerous untruths are truths moderately distorted.

— Georg Christoph Lichtenberg

1

For the third time in a row, my phone call to my best friend Ahanti went to voicemail.

My trip to Washington, DC, with Mark to consider the job he'd been offered wasn't starting out the way we'd planned.

I knocked on her apartment door again. Ahanti never went anywhere without her cell. If she forgot it, she turned back, even if it meant she'd be late to an appointment. So she was either in her apartment and something was wrong, or she was out somewhere...and something was wrong. I'd been trying to reach her since our plane landed at Dulles International Airport hours ago. She couldn't possibly be asleep or indisposed for this long.

Mark leaned against the wall next to the door. "I know what you're thinking. Would it help if I promised you she's not dead?"

I shifted the phone to my other hand and contemplated dialing again. Mark was right. He did know what I was thinking. Not only because he knew me better than anyone else and because I apparently had an expressive face, but also because I'd ended up in the middle of more murders than anyone other than a serial killer should ever see in a year. It'd made me a little paranoid.

"You can't promise me that."

He gently removed my phone from my grip and tucked it back into my purse. "No, but the odds are in my favor. It's more likely she went out of town."

Perhaps. But if she'd gone somewhere, it'd be the first time in years that she'd done it without telling me. Even though I wasn't her designated next-door plant waterer anymore, she'd still told me when she and Geoff went to the Dominican over Christmas and headed down to Florida to spend Easter with his parents.

Relationships did change over time, though. I just hadn't expected it to happen to Ahanti and me. Since I'd moved to Michigan, we'd talked weekly and texted more often than that. I was supposed to be in her wedding next spring, and we'd stopped by her apartment so I could ask her in person to be in our wedding party. Since Mark wanted his two brothers as his co-best men, I'd planned to ask Ahanti to be co-maid of honor along with Mark's cousin Elise.

A trip did seem more likely than the macabre alternatives running through my head. I took the hand Mark offered me and let him lead me back to the elevator.

The unanswered calls continued to nag at me like an itch out of my reach. They weren't the only recent difference. "She didn't reply to my text saying we were coming down for a couple of weeks, either," I said softly.

Mark hit the button for the ground level, and the elevator doors dinged shut. "That only lends support to the theory that she's off somewhere. She's probably been gone since last week."

He sounded a little less certain than before.

"Is there someone you could call to check?" His hand tightened around mine. "Not that I think there's something wrong. Just so you can set your mind at ease."

Ahanti's relationship with her family was civil, but I wouldn't have called it close. They didn't approve of her career as a tattoo artist any more than my parents supported my move to Michigan to take over my Uncle Stan's maple syrup farm. She was supposed to be a doctor, like I was supposed to be a lawyer. Navigating the expectations of our families, alongside figuring out what we wanted from life, had been one of the things we bonded over.

I doubted her family knew when she was in the city and when she wasn't. Geoff would know. If I couldn't get him, either, then I could relax knowing they'd taken off on a trip together.

The elevator doors opened, letting us off in the lobby of the apartment complex. I wiggled my phone back out of my purse and trusted Mark to keep me from running into anything or anyone.

I didn't know Geoff's cell number, but since it was Monday, he should be at work. That number I still remembered. Geoff was my chiropractor when I lived in DC. Ahanti and I ran into him at the movies one night, I'd invited him to sit with us since he was there alone, and they'd been together ever since.

His receptionist answered, but she wasn't the one who'd been with him when I'd gone there. Not surprising, since his original had been close to retirement.

The new receptionist confirmed that he was in the office. I gave her my name, told her I was a friend of Geoff's, and said I'd wait if he was with a patient.

The hold tone beeped in my ear all the way out to our rental car. We climbed inside, and Mark started the car, cranking the air conditioning against the oven-like late-June sun. He didn't put the car into drive.

"Nicole?" Geoff's voice came through the phone. "Is everything alright?"

That was a weird reaction. Granted, I didn't normally call him at work now that I wasn't his patient, but the tone of his voice was shock to hear from me rather than surprise.

This could all have a simple explanation. Maybe Ahanti's phone wasn't working and she didn't realize it yet.

Maybe she hadn't even gotten my text. Maybe Geoff didn't know I was in town for a visit.

"Everything's fine." No need to advertise I'd let my anxiety get the best of me. "Didn't Ahanti tell you I was coming down? I've been trying to call her, but I kept getting her voicemail. I thought we could all get together for dinner or something."

The pause on his end stretched, and my ribs started to ache. It took me a second to realize I was holding my breath. I let the air out and sucked in a fresh gulp.

"I think she might have changed her number," he finally said.

My heart felt like I'd been sucked back in time, back to the teenage girl I'd once been who hadn't been asked to the prom. Why wouldn't Ahanti have told me if she changed her number? Ahanti had never been the type to be easily insulted, and I couldn't think of anything I'd done to make her this angry, but it felt like Geoff was holding back. Almost like Ahanti had asked him not to give me her new number.

"You're not sure if your fiancée changed her phone number?" I asked carefully, trying desperately to control the snark that wanted to creep into my tone.

"She broke up with me a week and a half ago. By text. I tried calling her a couple of times, saying we needed to talk about it. I got another text telling me that if I didn't stop calling, she was going to change her number."

I mouthed the words *holy crap* to Mark. My mouth was

probably hanging open so wide we could have hid valuables in it.

"I don't know if she actually did or not." A ragged edge sneaked into Geoff's voice.

None of this made any sense. A few weeks ago, Ahanti was texting me links to strapless wedding dresses that would show off her tattoos, and we were joking about the best spring honeymoon destinations. She'd been all puppy dog eyes and *he's my soulmate* over Geoff practically since they met. They'd been hunting for an apartment near her studio that would be big enough for both of them to live in since Ahanti's studio apartment was too small to fit all Geoff's stuff, and she really wanted to stay within walking distance from work.

"I'm surprised she didn't tell you," Geoff said.

"Me too." At least he'd gotten a Dear John text. That was more than I'd gotten. Which didn't fit, either. Why dump her boyfriend and her best friend all in the span of a couple of weeks? She was too young for a mid-life crisis. The anxious feeling crawled back up into my throat. "Did she seem okay to you before she called it off?"

He sighed, and it sounded like a shrug. "I don't know anymore. She was stressed out, but I thought that was normal wedding planning and apartment hunting jitters."

That might well be all it was. Ahanti could etch permanent ink onto a person's face without so much as a hand tremor, but every year around tax time, she'd practically end up curled up in the fetal position around a bottle of wine.

Still, in her meltdown moments, she was the kind of person to hold her loved ones closer rather than push them away.

"Do you think it could be something else?" Geoff asked, fear and hope mingling together in his voice. "I never would have expected her to cut you off."

I could have said the same thing about him. Actually, I should. I knew too well what he must be going through.

"Same with you. I'm only here for a bit, but I'll try to track her down in person and get some answers." If all else failed, I had resources for it that Geoff didn't. My parents had a whole cadre of private investigators on speed dial. At least one of them had to be free from casework at the moment and willing to make some money from a different Fitzhenry-Dawes. Hopefully it wouldn't come to that, though. "Did you try meeting up with her at her studio?"

"Yeah, but some big dude blocked the door and told me I wasn't welcome inside."

Given that she hadn't responded to my attempts at contact, I might very well receive the same reception. She wouldn't recognize Mark as easily. That was another ace in my hand if I needed it.

Since today was Monday, Ahanti's studio was closed. It'd be at least tomorrow before we could swing by. "I'll let you know once I've talked to her."

"Thanks, Nicole," he said softly. "I've been worried about her."

I disconnected the call. Mark had angled in his seat so that he leaned back against the driver's door, watching me.

I felt a bit like a specimen in an experiment. "What?"

His gaze moved over my face. "I figured something out about you."

My best friend had dropped her fiancé and me in one clean-slate wipe. There were no guarantees that Mark wouldn't have a lightbulb moment one day and realize that I wasn't what he wanted after all. We'd known each other less time than Ahanti and Geoff had, after all. "I'm not sure I like the sound of that."

"When we talked about it before, you made it sound like the puzzle was why you kept getting involved in cases even when it was dangerous. I don't think that's it. At least not all of it."

I gave him a sidelong *do tell* look. If I'd had his unnatural eyebrow control, I would have quirked one at him.

"You're the opposite of the Grinch," he said. "Your heart is three sizes too large."

I snorted. If you asked my dad, that was my biggest failing. But I was pretty sure Mark didn't feel the same way. "Endearing or annoying quality?"

One of his dimples peeked out. "A little of both. But mostly endearing. At least I know there's plenty of room in that heart for me." He shifted in his seat and put the car into drive. "Now, since I know we'll be trying to track down Ahanti before our meeting tomorrow with my new potential boss, how about you show me some of the sights today?"

2

*T*he next morning, Mark parked in a lot down the street from Ahanti's tattoo parlor, Skin Canvas. Since I'd moved to Fair Haven, we'd had a running joke about what she'd have to rename it if she relocated there. Our top two picks had been Just Ink About It and INKcredible Tattoos.

It was a strange feeling now walking up to her studio and not knowing if I'd be welcome or not. My sandals felt like they were sticking to the asphalt for more reasons than just the scorching sun.

Mark and I had discussed it on the way there. I'd try to go in, and if no one stopped me, then he'd follow along. It'd be better if I could talk to Ahanti myself. If Ahanti put the same human barricade in place for me as she had for Geoff, then Mark would hang back and enter under the guise of being a potential customer.

A glance through the window showed Ahanti's co-artist Terrance working on a woman's wrist. No Ahanti, and no human meat shield in sight.

I went in with Mark close behind. The first time I'd visited Ahanti's tattoo parlor, I'd expected someplace dark and kind of grungy, with dim lighting and an aroma of cigarette smoke and booze. I hadn't been good at hiding the expectation, either. The first thing out of my mouth when I'd walked through the doors that first day into the bright, sterile environment was *It's so clean!* It even smelled nice thanks to the bowls of lavender potpourri Ahanti kept around.

Thankfully, Ahanti hadn't taken my reaction personally. She'd had a few stereotypes about lawyers that we'd had to break through, too, in our early days of friendship.

Terrance glanced up. With his head out of the way, I got a better look at the design he was working on—another biomechanical piece, his specialty. He'd made the woman's skin look like it was peeling back to reveal a mechanical arm underneath.

"Hey, Nicole. You in town for a visit? Ahanti's in the back."

His gaze was already on his work again before he finished speaking. He was one of those people who asked questions, but then didn't actually wait for you to answer them. When I used to hang out in the studio while Ahanti worked on designs for clients, that particular quirk of Terrance's used to make my skin crawl. Turned out I hadn't built up an immunity to it in my time away. It still made me want to slap tape over his mouth as soon as he asked a question so I'd be able to respond.

As if she'd heard her name, Ahanti came through the back-room door, a bottle of red ink in her hand. She wore a mint-colored vintage flapper dress and was as long and lean as ever, but the bright blue streak in her hair showed dark roots at the bottom. I'd never seen her leave it the same color long enough for the roots to grow out before.

She stopped one step through the doorway, and her hand clenched around the ink bottle. For an awkwardly long time, we stood and stared at each other. I wanted to run to her for a hug, and she looked like she wanted to run away.

She licked her lips. "Unless you're here for a tattoo, you'll have to leave."

She completely ignored Mark as if she didn't even see him. Either that, or she'd figured out who he was, and her dismissal included him as well.

Terrance's gaze hopped to Ahanti, then back to his work. A tiny frown formed between his eyebrows, and he leaned closer over his client's arm.

Mark wandered a little bit away and acted like he was interested in the photos on the walls of some of Ahanti's more intricate designs. He stayed close enough to eavesdrop, but far enough away to be unthreatening to Ahanti.

All the things I'd planned to say fell out of my mind and rolled across the floor and out of reach. A large part of me had believed that, once Ahanti saw me here in person, she'd throw open her arms and tell me exactly what was going on.

Now I had no doubt that she'd gotten my messages and had chosen to ignore them.

That still didn't tell me why.

Terrance's client was openly gawking, and whatever was going on, I doubted Ahanti would discuss it in front of a client. The tattoo parlor didn't have quite the same one-sided stereotypical dynamic of a bartender with a customer, but it did have a lot more in common with a beauty salon than most people probably realized. Tattoo artists often filled the role of listening ear and unofficial therapist for their clients, which meant they weren't as forthcoming with their own personal lives. Clients wanted to unburden, not take on the added burden of whatever was happening in their artist's life.

"Could we talk in the back?" I asked.

Her fingers tapped against her leg. "We don't need to talk. If you'd like to see a book of past designs, I'd be happy to set you up with that." She gestured toward two plush chairs off to the side. "But we only do custom work, and we don't take walk-ins."

This conversation had to sound strange to anyone listening. I clearly knew her, and she was acting like I was some gawker off the street. I moved closer and lowered my voice. "I talked to Geoff. He's worried about you, and so am I."

Something flickered across her eyes—there and gone before I could figure out what it was. "Noted, but I know what I'm doing."

I know what I'm doing rather than *I'm fine*. Maybe it was my paranoia rearing up again and making me see dangers and cries for help where there weren't any, but that struck me as a deliberate choice of words.

"I can help." I kept my response sub-vocal, trusting her to read my lips. "Is something wrong?"

She set the ink down on the counter. "I know letting go of an old friendship can be hard, but people change, and it's time to move on. I don't have time for a long-distance thing."

Her expression stayed neutral. If she needed help, if something was wrong that she felt like she couldn't talk about here, she could have given me some sort of tiny signal. She didn't.

I turned for the door. I felt more than saw Mark fall into step behind me. His hand slid gently onto the small of my back as we headed out the door.

"If that's your best friend," he said once the door closed behind us, "I hope we don't run into any of your old enemies."

He meant it as a joke to take the edge off the sting, I knew. That was the Cavanaugh way. The lump filling my throat kept me from answering.

She sounded like she was fine and had decided she wanted a different life than the one she had. Like she'd decided, as abruptly as she'd decided she was done with Geoff, that my friendship wasn't worth the effort.

~

A BMW SWERVED IN FRONT OF US, NEARLY CLIPPING OUR front bumper. It wasn't the first.

Mark laid on the horn and let slip a curse word. He glanced over at me. "Sorry. That guy doesn't know how to drive."

In the few minutes it'd taken us to drive from M Street to Georgetown University, I'd watched Mark transform from mild-mannered Dr. Cavanaugh into road-rage filled Mr. Hyde. He gripped the steering wheel so tightly that the bones in his hands stood out in harsh lines.

This trip was turning out to be a learning experience for both of us. "I thought I didn't like DC traffic, but you've got me beat."

The look Mark shot me was the closet I'd ever seen him come to scowling at me. "If we move here, we need to live near public transit."

"You didn't have a car in New York?"

He shook his head. "I'll have an ulcer within a month if I have to drive in this every day."

I decided that this was one of the few times I probably shouldn't tease him. I hadn't actually minded the traffic that much when I lived here, but that was because I used the time to listen to audio books. A good story made bad traffic much more tolerable. We could find a place with convenient public transit for Mark, and I'd battle the traffic to work.

The GPS told us to take the next exit, and we were soon safely parked. Despite the traffic, we were even five minutes early. The change in Mark as soon as he shut the car off was visible. The hard edges came out of his jaw, and the color returned to his hands.

He stepped out of the car the way a seasick person steps off a boat onto solid land. "I'd suggest you drive us back to the hotel, but I know your driving record."

I stuck my tongue out at him. "Hardy har har. For your information, I didn't have a single accident here."

He grabbed my hand and brushed a kiss across my knuckles before we headed inside.

The tour almost made me forget Ahanti's rejection, the horrible traffic, and the impending dinner with my parents.

The lab was exactly what I'd expected from a research grant, but the people—it was like we'd been on an alien planet and we were returning home. The team leader met us in the lobby, wearing a t-shirt with a math joke on it under his lab coat.

"Worth the drive," I whispered to Mark at one point.

I got the full force of his dimples in response.

My heart felt cleaved down the middle. If he wanted this job, I'd come back here for his sake, but it held a lot less appeal now. Most of my so-called friends from when

I'd previously lived in DC turned out to not be interested in keeping in touch when I went from lawyer to maple syrup farm owner. Ahanti had been one of the few who stuck by me.

My steps slowed even though Mark and the team leader continued on.

I don't have time for a long-distance thing, Ahanti had said.

But I'd already told her we might be moving back. She must have been betting on me realizing that what would sound like a brush off to anyone listening was exactly the opposite.

It was a silent cry for help.

3

*W*hat kind of trouble had Ahanti gotten into that she was afraid of speaking freely even in her own studio? And that she'd feel the need to cut off her fiancé and me? I had to assume now that she'd done it to protect us.

Mark came back around the corner, clearly wondering where I'd disappeared to.

I spackled on a smile. No matter my suspicions about Ahanti's situation, I wasn't going to ruin this for Mark. We couldn't do anything until the tour was done anyway. "There was an intersection, and I didn't have a GPS."

One of our running jokes was how I had a special skill for getting lost. Hopefully that'd stall him from asking more questions at least.

The look he gave me said he didn't quite believe me, but

he took my hand anyway, and we caught back up with the team leader.

The rest of the tour only solidified in my mind that Mark would be happy if he decided to take the job. I doubted that would change after he got a closer look over the next week at the research they were doing.

By the time we got lunch in the cafeteria, though, I felt like a kid at the end of a long drive.

Mark slid his tray onto the table and took the chair next to me. "You have that look on your face like you're desperate to tell me something."

I'd planned to at least wait until we were out of the building, but now that he'd asked, if I didn't tell him, he'd probably worry that I was holding back something about the job. I filled him in on my revelation.

"Are you sure it's not just wishful thinking?"

It might be, but there was only one way to find out. "I think I should talk to her."

"You already talked to her."

"We weren't alone in her studio."

Mark steepled an eyebrow. "You think she was afraid of her employee or the woman getting a tattoo?"

Not likely. Terrance had worked with Ahanti since she opened her tattoo parlor. If she'd been afraid of the woman customer, she could have waited until she left and then called me. For that matter, she could have emailed or texted me today, yesterday, or any time in the past week.

Mark was probably right. It certainly sounded more

reasonable than my grasping at what could have been simply me overanalyzing Ahanti's choice of words.

But she'd been my best friend for so long. She'd stuck by me through having my heart broken by a married man and changing careers and all manner of other things. If there was even a chance that this wasn't what it seemed, I couldn't abandon her. "I need to do this."

"Not by yourself." Mark took the final swig of his soda, then piled all his trash onto the tray. "If we're going to do this, we need to figure out how to contact her in a way she'll feel safe responding to."

Good Lord, I loved this man.

∾

WE STILL DIDN'T HAVE A PLAN BY THE TIME WE NEEDED TO leave for dinner with my parents. Working on the assumption that she didn't feel comfortable telling me what was going on using her phone or email or talking to me in person, it wasn't as simple as sending her a message through one of those means.

Mark had suggested sliding a letter under her apartment door, but I knew from living there that there wasn't a gap under the door to slide anything. If we mailed a letter, it might not reach her before we left.

"What about taping it to her door?" Mark asked. We were out of the worst of the traffic, so he'd relaxed his death grip on the wheel.

"If she's so worried about someone intercepting her communication, I'm not comfortable being so obvious about it."

I'd hate to cause Ahanti more trouble than she was already in if this was more than her deciding to make drastic changes in her life for the sake of change.

Mark parallel parked on the street in front of my parents' building. My parents could have easily afforded a house, but their apartment came with a superintendent and no need to upkeep a yard—or hire someone to do it. They'd never had much patience for anything that could interfere with their work time or their very limited leisure time. Besides, you could see the Washington Monument while swimming in the rooftop pool. Very few locales could boast that kind of a view. The waiting list for an apartment in their building could be two years or more.

My mom buzzed us in, and my head felt a bit like I'd been given a dose of anesthetic—all fuzzy and disconnected. Assuming my dad spoke to me today, it'd be the first time in five months. Whether the silence was still anger-motivated or he thought he could shame me into coming back, I wasn't sure. My mom didn't even seem to know. According to her, my dad didn't want to speak *about* me any more than he wanted to speak *to* me.

The elevator ride and walk down the hall to my parents' apartment felt a bit like walking the plank. Or at least what walking the plank would have felt like if pirates had actually killed people that way. Shooting their prisoners or running them through with a sword was more efficient, granted, but if making them suffer before death had been a goal, I could see this as a good way to go.

"You're not going to pass out on me, are you?" Mark asked. "It'd be a shame if you crushed the cheesecake after we brought it all the way here."

Nancy, my go-to person for all things food-related, had baked and packaged the maple syrup cheesecake for me to bring to my parents. I'd wanted some way to display Sugarwood's product, and TSA restrictions meant I couldn't carry a bottle of maple syrup on the plane with me, and packing it in my luggage would have given me nightmares about broken bottles and ruined clothes. The cheesecake I'd been able to carry on and tuck under my seat on the plane.

I tried to move my lips into a smile for Mark's sake, but I had a feeling it came out more like a crazed grimace. "I won't pass out. My dad would see that as weakness."

I did let Mark knock on the door, though. With the way my hands were shaking, I wasn't sure I could safely hold the cheesecake in one hand or that I'd knock loud enough for them to even hear me.

Mark's knuckles had barely hit the wood before the door swung open, almost like they'd been waiting even though we were a couple of minutes early. I wouldn't have dared be late.

I'd seen my mom only a few weeks earlier. Today she had the worn-down look in her eyes that she only got when she was working a tough case that required too many "needless" battles for information and way too many cups of coffee. Cases usually energized my parents, but one of my mom's pet peeves was having to fight to get information that should have been provided to her as normal operating procedure.

My dad stood slightly behind her. Same Armani suit, wrinkle-free even after a day at work, as if he'd changed it before we arrived. He actually might have. First impressions, according to my dad, were worth ten eloquent arguments. His clients didn't set foot in the courtroom without him approving every element of their appearance.

But instead of a scowl, he wore a smile.

I blinked rapidly, but it wasn't an illusion. The smile was still there.

He extended a hand to Mark, but I barely caught his greeting. My mom had promised to talk to him on my behalf. Maybe she'd succeeded. Maybe I'd been worried for nothing.

When he turned his gaze in my direction, it reminded me of sapphires, warm on the outside but hard to the touch.

He hadn't forgiven me. But first impressions were everything, and this was the first time he'd met Mark— whose good reputation I was sure my mom had ensured proceeded him.

The table was already set with the food laid out. Anyone else might have been worried we'd be late and the meal would grow cold, but not my parents. Because I knew better than to be late. They'd raised me, after all.

I recognized the meal on the first bites of heirloom baby carrots and pommes aligot as coming from one of my parents' favorite fine dining restaurants. Just like they never cleaned, and never repaired anything that broke, they also never cooked a meal. My mom had a shelf of cookbooks in the kitchen, suggesting she'd known her way around the kitchen at one time, but that time had long passed before I entered high school.

Hearing Ahanti's name snapped me back to the conversation. It'd been a man's voice. I couldn't imagine Mark telling my parents that Ahanti had "dumped" me as a friend.

It sounded like my dad was telling the story of how Ahanti helped save my life when Peter tried to kill me.

My dad shifted his gaze in my direction again, and it took everything I had not to shrink under the force of it. It was the look he normally reserved for the prosecution after he finished a line of questioning with a witness. The one that said *Only a fool would contradict me.*

"Her mother and I understand that, after an experience like that, almost anyone would need time away. We've only ever wanted what's best for her, and we're glad you'll be moving back to DC so she can return to her career."

It was a statement packed with messages. The one for me said, *If you come back, all will be forgiven and we'll never speak of this again.* The one for Mark was the kind of pressure my dad was so good at exerting—a subtle implication that if we didn't come back, he'd be holding me back and sabotaging my life.

The worst of it was, my dad probably knew exactly what he was doing. My mom would have told him enough about my relationship with Mark for him to know that Mark would do much more than move partway across the country if it was what was best for me.

A little ball of heat formed in my chest. I imagined it growing until I could shoot fire like a dragon. "We haven't decided whether we're moving back or not. We both have careers we enjoy in Fair Haven, so it's not a decision to be made lightly."

"Nicole." My mom rose to her feet. "Could you help me with the dessert?"

The expression that flickered across her face worked as well as a bucket of ice water in putting out my anger. It almost looked like sadness. I hadn't considered before that the strained relationship I had with my dad might negatively affect my mom.

I gathered up the empty plates and followed her into the kitchen without argument.

I hadn't been wrong in what I'd said, but I probably shouldn't have said it. I could have told Mark later to ignore him, that it'd been my choice to move to Fair Haven, and that my career wasn't any more or less important than his. "I'm sorry, Mom."

My mom barely acknowledged. Apologies were another thing that weren't done in our family.

She pulled a white paper bag from the refrigerator and tucked the leftovers back inside. As I'd expected, the logo for the upscale restaurant they liked was emblazoned across the bag. So upscale that they technically called it catering rather than takeout. My tastes had never been as fancy once I moved out on my own, even before Fair Haven. Ahanti and I used to order Chinese and sit on one of our couches to eat it straight out of the containers.

That was it!

Only the knife I held to cut the cheesecake kept me from fist pumping the air. I could go to the Chinese restaurant we always used to order from, place an order for delivery, and request to put a note inside before it went out. That's how I could communicate with Ahanti.

4

I leaned forward, pretending I wanted a better look at the painting on the wall in front of me. In my Chinese-food note the night before, I'd asked Ahanti to meet us in the section of the National Gallery of Art where they displayed seventeenth-century Dutch and Flemish works. I knew from past visits that it was never as busy as the special exhibits or any of the areas dedicated to the artwork by the Italian masters.

It was also the only place I could think of where we'd be hard to spot, have to go through a security checkpoint before we came in, and Ahanti would have a reasonable excuse for leaving her phone in her car. While phones weren't prohibited, photography was for certain collections, and loud conversations were strongly frowned upon. Ahanti would have normally brought her phone anyway, but I'd suggested in my note that she conveniently forget it.

My cell phone beeped with a text notification. Maybe Ahanti had decided a text was worth the risk and wanted to meet somewhere else. I grabbed for my phone so fast I almost shot it out of my hands and across the room.

The message wasn't from Ahanti. It was from Mandy. Since I'd helped her when a murder happened at her bed-and-breakfast last month, she'd insisted on being the one who watched Velma and Toby while Mark and I were out of town. My business partner, Russ, would have been the better choice since Mandy would probably spoil both dogs, but I hadn't been able to find a way to tell Mandy that that wouldn't have hurt her feelings.

Do I have to use the leather leashes? Mandy wrote. *They're ugly, and you have nicer purple and blue ones.*

I'd left two pages of instructions about the dogs in the hope that Mandy wouldn't explode my phone with questions while I was gone. I should have known better. How the heck she'd ever found those colored leashes was beyond me. I'd set out the leather ones, and the last time I saw the nylon ones, they'd fallen behind the food bag.

If you don't want to burn your hands, yes, I typed back.

I'd bought the pretty nylon leashes before I signed Velma up for obedience classes. At the very first introductory session, before we even brought our dogs with us, the instructor banned the kind of leashes I had because of how painful it could be if our dog yanked it through our hand.

I pocketed my phone again and moved on to the next painting.

Mark moved along with me. "How long past the meet time do we wait?"

I checked my watch. The meet time I'd written on my note passed ten minutes ago. Given DC-area traffic, ten minutes late wasn't terrible. And we had no way of knowing what her appointments had been like for today. For all we knew, she'd had one she couldn't reschedule or the one ahead ran long.

Ahanti came around a corner, and my shrug stalled out halfway up. I could tell the moment she spotted us because she veered sharply in our direction.

She walked straight into a hug. "Only you would think to hide a note in a bag of takeout."

I didn't have to be a lawyer or a police officer to identify the relief in her voice. It matched what I felt inside. I'd been right.

Then, just as quickly, I felt like a selfish jerk. I probably shouldn't feel relieved that something was wrong rather than that she didn't want to be my friend anymore, but I had to hope that whatever was wrong, we could fix. If she'd truly wanted to end our friendship, there'd have been nothing I could do.

"What's going on?" I asked. "I'm not the only one who's worried about you. I talked to Geoff when I got into town."

There was a tremor in her hand as she brought it up to run through her hair. A matching shiver skittered over my skin. Ahanti's hands never shook.

"I didn't know any other way to keep him safe. Both of

you safe." She glanced back over her shoulder, like even now she expected someone to be watching or listening. "Two weeks ago, someone left a picture of Geoff and me on my desk in the back room. They'd burned out his face and wrote *I love you more* across the back."

I leaned into Mark's solid arm for support. "You broke up with Geoff to protect him."

She nodded. "I did some reading about stalkers online, and a lot of what I saw made it sound like if whoever did this thought I belonged to him, he might hurt Geoff to *save* me from him, or some warped thinking like that."

The sad part of my parents' business was that we dealt with the perpetrators rather than the victims. I'd been on the defense counsel side of a couple stalking cases. Ahanti's fears were justified. Stalkers could become violent to both the object of their obsession and anyone who stood between them and what they wanted from the person they were stalking.

They didn't normally jump straight into this level of contact, though. They tended to escalate. It should have started with something much smaller.

Ahanti hadn't told me about anything, either recently or back when we were neighbors. At least, not that I could recall. "Is this the first thing that's happened that made you think you have a stalker?"

She drew in a long breath, and it came out shaky. "The other stuff seemed innocent. It was mostly little gifts left at the studio. I get thank-you cards from clients sometimes, when I've helped them cover up a scar or hide an old tattoo of an ex's name. I didn't think the gifts were weird even though the cards were a bit personal." She made an I-don't-get-it gesture. "You've been there. We spend hours, sometimes days, working with clients. It's easy to feel connected after that amount of time. People share all kinds of personal details. It's not the first time I had a client feel like we were friends or even ask me out."

I bit the inside of my cheek. Crap. She had told me all that. She'd even shown me a couple of the cards. We'd thought it was harmless and sweet. At one point, we'd even thought some of them might be from Geoff. I should have known better. Me, of all people. "Was the photo the only thing that seemed threatening?"

Ahanti's gaze dropped.

My hand clenched around Mark's arm. The gesture was so out of character for her, as if she thought she'd done something wrong.

"Some of the more recent notes mentioned things he shouldn't have known about. One sounded almost like something I'd written in an email to you. The other was something I was sure I'd only told Geoff in a phone call."

That explained why she'd been too afraid to use her phone or computer to tell me what was going on. Her stalker seemed to have somehow tapped into her private communications. Since the stalker was sending things to the studio, that also explained why she'd been afraid to say anything while we were there. Right now, we had no idea how he accessed her private communications. He could have bugged her studio or hacked her email. Maybe both.

Unfortunately, if he was tech-savvy enough, he might have even hacked her phone or put a keystroke tracker on her computer. As technology progressed, criminals were progressing right along with it.

I took her hand to make sure I had her attention. "You know this isn't your fault, right?"

She raised her shoulders in a noncommittal shrug. "I must have encouraged him somehow, or this wouldn't be happening."

It was a common misconception about stalking cases that didn't involve a celebrity. Many people assumed that the victim led the perpetrator on in some way and was partly culpable for what was happening to them. Nothing could be further from the truth. And it didn't help that, at times, some movies and books portrayed stalking behavior as romantic. When *Twilight* was a craze, I was never able to get past how creepy Edward's behavior seemed. Even then, I'd seen too much of the dark side to ever be that innocent again. Since my parents never sheltered me, I don't think I was ever really innocent, even as a child.

The fact that Ahanti would even think she was partly to blame reminded me of the case I'd been part of only a couple of weeks ago. Blaming the victim had eventually led to the victims becoming murderers themselves. "You're no more to blame than a woman who's been raped."

She adjusted the strap of the bag she had slung across

her chest. It reminded me of a soldier strapping on his weapon for battle. And it looked a lot more like the Ahanti I knew.

"So is there something I can do about it?" she asked.

Mark held his phone out to her. "First, I think you should call your fiancé." He glanced at me. "He deserves to know what's going on."

He didn't have to say *it's what I would want.* I heard it, and Ahanti must have, too, because she accepted the phone from him.

"And then," Mark said, "we're going to the police."

~

AN HOUR AND A HALF LATER, AHANTI AND I SAT IN THE nearest Metropolitan Police station. Because the stalker sent his "love notes" to Skin Canvas and that was in their jurisdiction, it seemed like as good a place as any to start.

By the time Ahanti had finished talking to Geoff and we'd taken her to buy a pay-as-you-go phone that the stalker wouldn't know about, Mark was barely going to have time to make his appointment at the lab. I told him we'd be fine to wait by ourselves to talk to an officer.

After all, even I couldn't get into too much trouble inside a police station. Not life-threatening trouble, anyway.

Ahanti and I waited in silence, the only break coming from another text. Mandy sent me a picture of a thick, raw-looking red line across a palm and the words *you were right*. She couldn't say I hadn't warned her.

Another five minutes passed, and Ahanti crossed and uncrossed her legs. "Maybe this isn't a good idea. I'm going to be away from work for most of the day. If he's watching my business, he'll know something's up."

Once we reported this, that was our next hurdle. Some stalking victims refused to change anything about their life, seeing that as a victory for their harasser. Others wanted to take every precaution to protect themselves in case the stalker lashed out, including moving.

"For all he knows, you had a doctor's appointment and forgot your phone. Or you felt sick and went home. Have you gotten anything at your apartment?"

Ahanti worried her bottom lip. "I don't think so. It's all come to Skin Canvas so far."

"Then it's likely he doesn't know where you live."

That was a bit of a stretch. He likely knew her building. He'd probably followed her on her walk home, but her building had a locking external door. You needed a key to get in or a resident had to buzz you in. Mark and I had gotten in the other day because one of my former neighbors recognized me and knew Ahanti and I were close. That meant it wasn't impossible for someone to gain access who shouldn't, but it would be hard, and Ahanti would have noticed if someone followed her right in and up to her floor.

We fell into silence. For the first time, I didn't know

what to say to Ahanti. All the things I'd planned to say, all the things I'd been looking forward to talking to her about, now seemed inappropriate for the situation.

Ahanti shot me a sideways glance, and the corners of her eyes crinkled like she had a smile inside that she wasn't sure whether to let out or not either. "Mark's nothing like Peter."

I laugh-snorted. If she could compliment Mark and take a jab at my ex-boyfriend at the same time, maybe I shouldn't have worried about what to say after all. It seemed like Ahanti wanted a bit of normal in the midst of it all. "That's an understatement."

"How'd it go with your dad?"

I held back a second snort. It was getting to be a bad habit I needed to quit. This time, though, I didn't feel like adding a laugh to it. "He seemed to like Mark."

"That bad?"

It hadn't really been. After our near argument prior to dessert, he'd been civil the rest of the evening. More than civil. If he'd been anyone else, I would have said he was amiable, so much so that Mark even commented on it afterward.

He was also up to something.

Mark hinted that I might be imagining things, but he had the good sense not to say it explicitly.

A detective with a nasal voice called Ahanti's name, and she clutched my arm like she thought I might stay behind. I hadn't even considered it.

My mom couldn't have known when she recommended Mark to the head of the forensic research program that she'd be putting me back in DC at the time Ahanti would need me. My pastor would call it God's timing.

The detective led us back to a desk with enough files and scattered papers piled on it that my fingers twitched to organize it for him. His coffee cup had what looked like a permanent ring around it on the desk.

Ahanti sat on the metal chair next to his desk. She stayed on the edge rather than settling in, her back so straight that her spine could have doubled as a measuring tape.

The detective snagged another empty chair from nearby for me.

Ahanti told him her story. When she reached the part about Geoff's burned-out face in the picture, she started to shake to the point where her teeth chattered. I finished the story for her, repeating back for the detective what she'd told Mark and me.

The detective pulled a tissue from the box on his desk and wiped it across his forehead even though the air conditioning kept the humidity outside at bay. He tossed the tissue into the trash near my feet. "If we knew who your stalker was, we could put a restraining order in place. The problem we're facing right now is that he's keeping himself hidden."

Ahanti was still looking at him like she expected there was a solution coming.

The tone of the detective's voice carried an apology. There wasn't a solution coming.

The detective drew out another tissue and dabbed his face again. "In cases like these, we can't allocate resources to investigate the stalker's identity. If he makes contact in any way where you see his face, even calls you on the phone so we could get a name from the number, you come back in and let us know. Until then, there's nothing we can do."

5

"I shouldn't have called Geoff," Ahanti said as soon as we crossed the dividing line between the chilled interior of the police station and the muggy sun outside.

I wanted to say something comforting or encouraging or brave, but everything I came up with in my head would have sounded trite to me had the roles been reversed and I was the one afraid for Mark's life.

Even with all the murder investigations I'd been a part of in the past ten months, none of them made me feel this way. In Peter's case, I'd always had a niggling doubt that he might not be as innocent as he wanted me to believe. With Uncle Stan, he was already gone before I got involved with hunting down the person who hurt him.

After those two, the victims had been strangers or people I barely knew. This time it was my best friend.

I couldn't help feeling like I'd given Ahanti false hope. Not only that, but she was still unprotected from someone sick enough to burn her fiancé's face out of a photo.

"He'll never believe the I'm-breaking-up-with-you thing again." Ahanti stopped in the middle of the sidewalk. "Will you talk to him? He might listen to you about how dangerous this could be for him."

If it was anyone other than Ahanti, he might take my word as a criminal defense attorney. In this situation, nothing was going to keep him away when she was in danger.

I motioned for her to follow me so that we weren't standing like human traffic cones in the middle of the sidewalk. "That's not a good plan. He might be in danger, but so are you. What we need is a plan to keep you both safe."

"I already have a decent security system in my apartment. Maybe I should head out of town for a bit."

Unless she wanted to move permanently, a vacation wasn't going to be much help. Her stalker had been infatuated with her this long, and she'd gone away on trips before. He'd be waiting when she got back. And we still wouldn't be any closer to figuring out who he was.

Even if she did move, she'd have no guarantees that he wouldn't simply follow her. It all depended on how deep he felt the connection to her was.

A man passed by us in the opposite direction close enough that he brushed against my purse and set it swinging.

Ahanti flinched away from him and looked back over her shoulder until he was well out of range to grab one of us.

It took all my self-control not to do the same. Paranoia and anxiety were my constant companions, but even when I'd lived in the DC area, I hadn't felt scared to walk alone in the daylight in the nicer parts of the city. Now I wanted to check for people following us in the storefront glass, and I wished I'd asked Mark to skip his meeting and stay with us.

And this guy wasn't even my stalker. We couldn't simply do nothing and hope this would go away. It wouldn't. One of the stalkers my parents were hired to defend had tried to kill the object of his obsession. They didn't all reach that point, but I didn't want to take that risk. I was certain Geoff and Ahanti wouldn't want to take that risk with her life, either.

Even a restraining order didn't guarantee the stalker would leave her alone, but if we had enough information on him to get one, she'd also at least know who to watch out for. Right now, every person we passed could be a threat.

It wasn't a good way to live. She'd be headed for an ulcer before she turned thirty-five.

"If the police can't help until we know who this guy is, then that's what we need to figure out. It's time for us to hunt him."

~

By the time we reached Ahanti's apartment building, I already regretted my use of the word *hunt*. Clearly I'd been too graphic in recounting my adventures in Fair Haven. After I made my statement about hunting down her stalker, Ahanti looked like she was going to throw up on my shoes.

"You promise I won't have to confront him?" Ahanti asked.

"I promise." Mark was already going to hate this idea enough without me doing anything to make myself threatening to Ahanti's stalker. "All we need to do is figure out who this guy is. We'll let the police handle it from there."

She fished around in her purse again, still struggling to find her key.

Even once she had a restraining order in place, she needed to take steps to protect herself. "Little tip. Try to make sure you always have your key out and ready before you reach the door."

I left out the *it's too easy an opportunity for your stalker to corner you otherwise.*

She shuddered. "I hate having to think about this."

I stuck out my hands, and she plopped her bag into my grip. It was nearly the size of a child's backpack and at least as heavy.

She held it open with her now-free hand and wiggled her key out from behind her sketch pad and case of graphite pencils. We'd been apart long enough that I forgot all the things she carried around with her.

Once inside the building, she headed for the elevator.

I touched her arm. "The stairs are probably better," I said softly. "In an elevator, there's no place to run."

Her skin took on a yellow tinge under her natural beautiful tanned skin tone.

"Right." She pivoted and headed for the stairwell. "Right."

I wanted to tell her this wouldn't be forever, but stalking laws were much too weak. Unless her stalker found someone else to fixate on, this might have to be her new normal.

Ahanti's apartment was exactly how I remembered it, albeit with a bit more clutter. Her drawing table still sat next to the window that let in the best natural light, her Faber Castell polychromos colored pencils and hand guard splayed out across it like she'd been in the middle of a project when she had to leave for work. Stacks of boxes, all labeled, lined the walls, and piles of papers grew like mold over her end tables.

Theoretically, her apartment might have been big enough for her and Geoff to share, but it would have required a massive purge first. Or renting a storage unit. Geoff had suggested the latter to her when they first got serious, but Ahanti had insisted that she needed to be able to access her sketches and other keepsakes without traveling across town.

She still didn't have a TV or a radio, but her laptop sat open on her coffee table, and her state-of-the-art printer—the kind that could print images on photo paper just as well as any photo place—still didn't have a speck of dust on it even though I could have written my name in the layer on her bookshelf.

I deadbolted the door behind us and closed the lid of her laptop. She'd left her phone in the console of her car, so if her stalker had hacked either, we should still be safe from his prying ears.

Ahanti flopped down on the couch. "So where do we start?"

I joined her. Even though we weren't investigating a murder—thankfully—investigating this shouldn't be that much different. "Have you noticed anyone acting strangely?"

The expression on Ahanti's face clearly said *do I look stupid?* "I would have told you about that already." She ruffled her long hair and sighed. "Sorry. I don't even know what would make someone do this. How am I supposed to know what behavior to watch for?"

As I well knew, anyone's behavior could look strange or guilty if you were watching closely enough.

Ahanti slumped back against the couch cushions. "When I was reading online at work, there were like five or six different kinds of stalkers. I don't even know how to start narrowing it down to which *kind* mine might be, let alone who."

Her voice was taking on her *taxes are due tomorrow and I haven't even started them yet* tone.

Odd as it was, this was my element in the same way that she created art on human flesh. I could guide her through this.

I opened the browser on my phone and held it out to her. "Show me the page you were looking at with the descriptions."

She tapped on my phone's screen and handed it back to me.

I swiveled so that she couldn't peek at the screen. "I'm going to read these. Don't overthink it. Just tell me if anyone immediately leaps to your mind when I describe how this might have started."

The website gave each type of stalker a label, but I didn't want Ahanti getting caught up on those. I wanted her to think about the way she might have first come into contact with her stalker and who might be showing any behaviors similar to the ones listed.

I skipped the one where the stalker was basically a predator who was profiling their victim in order to sexually assault them. While Ahanti's stalker could technically be that, it didn't seem to fit with what she'd told me. Plus, I didn't need to scare her any more than she already was by even putting the thought in her mind.

I read her the description of the next type.

She was shaking her head almost before I finished. "That sounds more like someone who's really awkward and doesn't realize that you can't keep following someone around until they agree to date you."

She was right. She'd have noticed someone who was that socially inept trying to make contact with her. The description also implied that they usually lost interest quickly, and Ahanti said her stalker had been making indirect contact for years, even though she hadn't recognized it as stalking at the time.

I moved on to the next one, a stalker who begins after the breakdown of a close relationship with their victim.

Ahanti's hands clenched on her knees. "That one reminds me of Cary. Cary Gilbert. The guy I apprenticed with."

By the time I met Ahanti, she already owned Skin Canvas. She'd mentioned that she broke with the man who apprenticed her because she found out he was stealing her designs. She'd never offered more information, and I hadn't pressed because the situation was clearly something she'd wanted to leave behind her. I'd assumed it was because she didn't want to slander him—even though it wouldn't have been slander because it was the truth.

Now, if we were going to either confirm he was her stalker or cross him off the list, we'd have to dig into their relationship.

Considering how circumspect she'd been about it in the past, she'd probably be more comfortable telling me the story without anyone else around. I checked my phone. No text yet. Mark should be another twenty or thirty minutes at least, which gave us plenty of time.

"What makes you think it might be Cary?"

Ahanti shoved to her feet and went over to her drawing table. She picked up a green pencil crayon and ran it through her fingers as if the touch of it soothed her. "Cary didn't want to take me on as an apprentice even though he'd done all my tats and he'd seen my artwork. He knew I had great design ideas. But he was already apprenticing Terrance, and he said he didn't need another one."

I stayed quiet. Any questions I needed to ask, I could ask later. Right now, she just needed to get the story out.

"He'd asked me out a couple of times, and so I said, jokingly, that for every hour he taught me, I'd go out with him the same amount. After a month, I stopped keeping count of the hours, and it was really good for a while. We even talked about moving in together."

I hadn't known their relationship was personal as well as professional.

Ahanti set the pencil crayon back on her drawing desk in the exact spot she'd picked it up from. The rest of her apartment might be a mess, but her "studio corner" was precise, just like her studio.

"Things went bad when clients started to come in requesting me instead of him. Even some of his longtime customers. Some of the things he said..." She pressed her fists into the desktop. "Like that I'd prostituted myself to get the job and that the only reason they were picking me over him was that I was probably screwing them, too."

She turned her back to the window and the sun backlit her dark hair, making her look a lot like she must have back then, young and vulnerable.

"I stayed with him anyway because I loved him, and I thought if I left, somehow it would prove him right. Then one of my regulars told me that he was copying my designs and passing them off as his own. That's when I packed up. Once I opened Skin Canvas, most of my clients followed, and even Terrance asked to come on board."

I read the description on the website again. Based on Ahanti's story, Cary could fit the profile. But only if he'd kept in touch. The trigger event for stalkers was always a fresh meeting or a fresh rejection, not something that happened to them years ago that they didn't react to at the time.

"He doesn't sound like the kind of guy to let your defection go easily."

Ahanti crossed her arms under her chest, a subconscious self-protective gesture. "He begged me to come back and swore he hadn't been filching my work. He even offered to make me a partner in the business. By then I'd realized I was happier without him."

That was still years ago. "Did he let it drop after that?"

"Mostly. Every once in a while, usually when business is slow for him, he'll come by Skin Canvas and suggest we amalgamate, but he hasn't suggested we personally get back together for years." She flashed me her old brash smile. "Not since Terrance and Eddie threw him out last time he started hitting on me. And I mean *threw* literally."

That could explain why he'd resorted to sending gifts and love notes instead. He sounded egocentric enough that he probably assumed Ahanti would know they were from him even though he'd left them unsigned.

There was one upside to all of this. "If he's your stalker, I don't think he'll actually follow through on his threat against Geoff."

She stepped away from her desk, closer to the couch. "Why's that?"

"Once you had him thrown out of your studio, he didn't threaten the guys who helped you, and he got less direct with his communication. He de-escalated."

My phone pinged. *I'm done playing with the lab's toys for the day. Ready for some supper?*

Supper? I checked my watch. We'd lost the whole day. I texted him back. "Mark's on his way. Will you be okay here tonight? You could always stay with me at the hotel. We have separate rooms."

She moved to a panel by the door and brushed it with her fingers. "I'll keep my door locked and alarm system on. I'll call you tomorrow to set up a time to look at all the stuff. Hopefully there's something that will help prove it's Cary that I missed noticing." She unlocked the deadbolt but kept her hand on the door. "If Cary's the one who's been sending me all the messages, how did he hack my phone and emails? When we worked together, he could barely touch the computer without it freezing. Terrance did all the techie stuff."

"He might have learned since then." It niggled at my mind like the beginning of a headache, though. He might have gotten more proficient over the years, but he hadn't likely reached hacker-level skills. "I'll ask my parents to have one of their private investigators look into Cary. Maybe he hired someone. They might even be able to catch him in the act."

I reached for the door handle, but Ahanti kept her hand firmly blocking access. "I can't afford a PI. I've put everything I had in savings into the wedding."

"Don't worry about it. My parents and I still owe you for saving my life last year." I hugged her. "Besides, that's what friends are for."

She let me out, and I listened for the deadbolt sliding into place behind me. Even once it clicked into place, I couldn't shake the weighted feeling along my shoulders and down through my chest, almost like my purse was made of iron.

Even though we had a good idea of who her stalker might be, and even though I knew from when I'd watered her plants when she went on vacation in the past that she did have a good security system, I felt like I was leaving her in the Roman colosseum and praying the lions' cages held.

6

*O*nce Mark picked me up, I took the coward's way out and called my mom's cell rather than my dad's to ask about borrowing one of the private investigators they kept on retainer. Unfortunately, her phone went to voicemail. I hung up without leaving a message. I could wait for my mom, but I wanted someone looking into Cary right away.

I straightened my shoulders despite the fact that my dad wouldn't be able to see me. My parents had always insisted that proper posture gave you confidence. Now was as good a time as any to test their theory.

I dialed my dad's number.

"Edward Dawes."

"It's Nicole. I have a...request."

I'd almost said favor, but a favor implied an inability on

one side and generosity on the other. A request suggested it was one equal talking to another.

My dad had never seen me as an equal, in intelligence or ability, and maybe that was part of why he reacted so poorly whenever I didn't do exactly what he wanted me to. Most parents and their children negotiated their relationship as their children grew so that their parents became advisors—sometimes even friends—but their children's independent decisions and life choices were respected. Or at least tolerated without resorting to the silent treatment. My dad and I had never made that transition. He'd been protecting me and directing me my entire life until I left for Fair Haven.

"I'm on my way to court," my dad said. "Make it quick."

It was better than a flat-out *no*.

I could make it sound like I was working a case, and I'd be guaranteed his agreement, but I didn't want to play his game. I wanted our relationship—if we were going to have one going forward—to be able to endure the truth.

"Ahanti has been having trouble with a stalker. I have a lead on who it might be, but I need a PI to run some checks and tail him for a few days to see if we're right. We need to get enough evidence for a restraining order."

"I don't know if we have anyone free, and I don't have time to check."

On someone who didn't know him as well, that brush-off might have worked. It didn't work on me. "I'm happy to call the office and have someone there check for me."

The ambient driving noises coming through my dad's Bluetooth eased off like he was slowing down for a turn or a toll booth. "The firm's resources aren't there for you to waste on non-cases."

I closed my eyes and drew in a stabilizing breath because what I wanted to do was blow a raspberry at him through the phone and hang up. Loudly. Right in his ear. The prideful part of me that I'd probably inherited from him felt like hanging up on him and paying for someone myself. But my parents vetted all their private investigators, and they only hired the best. I needed the best.

Mark brushed a steadying hand against my shoulder.

I opened my eyes. I'd given my dad a chance to be generous. Now I'd have to show him that, however low his opinion of me was, I was still his daughter, and I was a stronger person than I'd once been. "Consider it repaying a debt then for the service Ahanti rendered us last fall."

The background noise picked up again in the time it took my dad to answer. "Call Caroline at the office. I assume you still know the number. And put Mark on."

Put Mark on? I covered the bottom of my phone with my hand. "He wants to talk to you," I whispered.

I fished the earbuds out of my purse, plugged them in, and outfitted Mark.

"Cavanaugh," he said, then winked at me. The man was smart.

"No," Mark said. "We don't have anything planned for tomorrow morning."

A pause.

"Okay, I'll be ready at six."

He motioned for me to take out the earbud. I disconnected the call.

Mark's mouth hung open slightly. "I've been summoned to go golfing with your dad tomorrow at his club."

Golf might be the game my dad invited Mark to, but he was definitely playing at something else. And, as always seemed to happen, I was left feeling like even though I'd won this encounter, I'd somehow played right into my dad's master plan.

SINCE MARK WOULD BE PLAYING GOLF WITH MY DAD AND having brunch at the club afterward, I had him drop me off at Ahanti's apartment so I could go with her to work. We had so little time to spend together, I wanted every moment I could grab.

Besides, until we could confirm that Cary was her stalker—and even once we had—we needed to look at ways to make her life safer.

The day didn't get off to quite the start we'd hoped, though. It took us longer to find a parking space than it would have to walk to Skin Canvas.

By the time we parked and headed inside, Ahanti had gnawed her bottom lip raw. I stayed quiet at her side. Driving had been my idea. I wouldn't be there to go home with her, and I'd insisted that she shouldn't be walking alone right now. Terrance could easily enough walk her out to her car, but it'd be asking a lot for him to walk her to and from work every day.

It'd seemed like a simple step she could take to protect herself, but I'd forgotten why she hadn't already moved across town into Geoff's apartment.

Walking to work had always been one of her joys, even in the winter and the heat stroke-inducing temperatures of summer.

I had to give her something else to focus on and give her a bit of hope. I hurried to keep up with her longer strides. "We could help tie Cary to that picture of Geoff if we could find someone who remembers seeing him here that day. Maybe you could make a list?"

Her lips relaxed back into a more normal shape. "I can check my appointment book for the customers."

Ahanti pulled the door open and didn't even pause at the fact that it was already unlocked. Even if she expected Terrance to have opened up and be inside, she should have checked more carefully anyway. It was something I'd need to talk about with her as well. But later.

Thankfully, this time, only Terrance stood at the back of the studio.

Ahanti flopped down in the chair next to Terrance's empty work station. "Was Cary in here two weeks ago?"

Terrance turned around, his gloved hands full of equipment he'd been pulling from the autoclave. "What'd he do now, steal something from us? Wouldn't surprise me if he had." He set the container down and started sorting the items. "He's always coming in here like he has some right to this studio because he trained us. He probably thinks he can take stuff to use without asking."

Terrance, clearly, was still as bad about answering questions as he was about giving anyone else a chance to answer them.

"You're going to have to be more specific," I whispered to Ahanti. "What day was it?"

Ahanti squirted a dollop of hand sanitizer into her palms and rubbed it over her hands as if she could protect herself from the whole situation as easily as she could germs. "Wednesday, Terrance. Did you see him in here two weeks ago yesterday?"

"Have we gone a whole week when he isn't in here? I know he showed up some day that week, but I don't remember which one it was."

That was probably the closest we were going to get to a definitive answer from Terrance. Really, I couldn't blame him for not remembering. If Cary were in here as often as it seemed, the days would blur together, especially with how many people came in and out of Skin Canvas on a daily basis. A client would be much more likely to remember who was also in and out during the time they were there.

I touched Ahanti's shoulder to signal she should stay put. "I'll grab you a paper and pen from the back so you can check the calendar for that day and write down who we need to contact. When's your first client scheduled for?"

"Unless I'm early," a soft voice said from behind me, "right now."

I spun around.

The man standing in the doorway was one of Ahanti's longtime clients. Since I'd seen him last, he'd shaved his head to strategically hide his receding hairline, but otherwise he looked exactly like I remembered. Same black t-shirt and blue jeans, as if he'd filled his closet with copies of the same clothes so that he never had to decide on what to wear. Same slight stoop to his shoulders as if he didn't want to be noticed for his six-foot stature.

"Eddie!" I smiled for what felt like the first time that day. "Long time no see."

He lumbered from the doorway into the studio, reminding me a bit of a bear in his movement. "Congratulations on your engagement."

Every time I heard Eddie speak, it surprised me that such a big man with such a deep voice could also keep his tone so soft.

I held out my hand to show him the ring. "We're planning a December wedding."

He nodded. Along with his soft voice, Eddie'd also never been one for small talk, though I knew from his many visits that he enjoyed a good conversation if someone else took the time to draw him out and show interest.

Ahanti was already on her feet. "I'll get your design from the back so we don't make you late for work."

I took the seat she'd vacated since it seemed strange to stand there staring up at Eddie. The last time I'd seen Eddie, almost a year ago now, he'd been in between jobs. "Sounds like I should congratulate you as well. Where are you working now?"

"My cousin started a security business. He wasn't gonna hire me since he thought it'd be uncomfortable working with family, but Ahanti convinced some of her clients to go with his company and insist on using me. He had to hire me then."

Terrance stuck his head around the corner. "Ed replaced the locks at my place."

Ahanti came back carrying her sketchbook. "And put the alarm pad into mine." Tension lines build around her mouth. "I'm glad to have it now."

Eddie didn't look at the sketchbook Ahanti opened on the table. "What's wrong?"

"It's Cary, isn't it?" Terrance's voice carried from the back room. "That's why you were asking about him coming in here."

Ahanti tightened her long ponytail and bobbed her head. Terrance wouldn't have been able to see her response. He probably wouldn't have been paying attention for an answer anyway.

"We think Cary's been..." She shook her head. "Doesn't matter. We're not even sure yet. But do you think you could come by and make sure my system's working the way it should? I want to be sure he can't get to me there."

That was another thing we'd talked about her doing. If her stalker was Cary, then he knew where she lived. If he couldn't get to her at work, a place he'd probably been using because it was the most convenient and easy access, he might try her home instead.

Eddie's face showed zero emotion. On anyone else, I'd have thought he didn't care, but Eddie never showed much emotion. I don't think I'd ever even seen him smile. And unlike Erik back home, who always seemed to be laughing underneath, Eddie seemed sad all the way down.

"I gotta be at work in a half hour, though," he said, "so I can't take care of it today. I'll give you a call."

Ahanti thanked him, and he took the sketchbook from her. I got a peek at it as it went.

The design seemed to be for a full back, based on the size and the fact that I knew Eddie already had an elaborate tribal design that wove around one of his arms and across his chest, leaving him without enough room for this one there. Ahanti had been touching that one up shortly before I'd gone to Fair Haven for Uncle Stan's funeral.

This one was of a wolf in a forest, howling at the moon. The moon wasn't an ordinary white. It was an orange harvest moon, and the wolf's eyes seemed to glow.

I wanted to snatch it from her, frame it, and display it.

Ahanti and I had never agreed on that. She'd always insisted she'd rather create art that lived with people rather than art they barely noticed in the rush of their lives. This piece had clearly been designed to be admired.

Handing it to Eddie, Ahanti looked the most at peace I'd seen her since I got back.

"Eddie let me choose the design this time," she said. "But it was really a joint project. He's given plenty of feedback along the way, and this hopefully will be the final sign-off before we start work."

Eddie handed the book back. "Whenever you can schedule me in."

They scheduled his first session, and he was gone with only a hand wave in goodbye.

Terrance watched him leave, a frown on his face. He rubbed his hand over his short, curly hair vigorously enough to give anyone who touched him a shock. "Did you drive here today, A? If Cary's hassling you again, you shouldn't be walking alone."

Ahanti's bottom lip dipped between her teeth again. If she chewed it much more, it'd start to bleed. "I drove."

"I'll park at your place and walk to and from with you a couple days a week if you want."

Ahanti squeezed his shoulder on her way past to the back room.

A shiver trickled over my upper arms, and I rubbed at the goosebumps. Terrance used to complain about the

Virginia heat. He and Ahanti were in a constant battle over the air conditioner settings in the studio.

He'd worked with Ahanti for longer than I'd known her, but I hadn't realized they were friends as well. Of course, you probably didn't stay working with someone that long unless you could also be friends. Or you were being paid a lot more than Ahanti made from Skin Canvas.

My phone rang. I didn't recognize the number, but it was Virginia-based. The only person here who had my new Michigan cell number and would be calling from someplace I didn't recognize was the private investigator my dad asked to look into Cary and watch Ahanti's place. I hadn't noticed him when we left this morning, which meant he was good. If it was the PI with news on Cary, I didn't want Ahanti to overhear. Her day was already off to a rough enough start.

I motioned to Terrance that I was going to take the call outside and stepped out the door. My skin instantly went tacky even though it wasn't yet nine o'clock.

"Nicole Fitzhenry-Dawes."

"My name's Lucas, Miss Fitzhenry-Dawes. I'm with Rockwood Investigations." The man's voice had a slight Hispanic accent. "I was told you were my contact when I had any information on the Ahanti Tenali case."

I'd been right to step outside.

A girl who looked to be around eighteen approached the door for Skin Canvas. I stepped out of her way and waited until the door closed behind her.

"That's right."

"There was a man lingering around her apartment building last night. I can't confirm his reason for being there yet. He made no contact. I got a picture of his license plate and face."

The air suddenly seemed too thick to breath. As much as we didn't want Cary anywhere near Ahanti if he turned out to be her stalker, this was the kind of thing we could take to the police to show he was.

"Was it the man in the photo we provided?"

"That's why I'm calling, ma'am. He wasn't. I kept a watch on him until he left this morning, but I wasn't sure if he was worth following or not."

That depended on whether or not Ahanti recognized him. We thought Cary was the best bet for her stalker, but we had no hard evidence. We couldn't cross off the possibility that it was someone else entirely.

"Could you text me the pictures?"

He confirmed that he would, and we ended the call. As soon as the pictures came in, I'd show them to Ahanti. If she knew him, we might want to change our focus.

My phone dinged, alerting me to a new text.

I tapped the message, and it opened on my screen.

My fingers suddenly felt unwieldy, like they'd swelled to twice their normal size. I didn't need to ask Ahanti if she recognized him. *I* recognized him.

It was Geoff.

7

I smoothed my hair and clothes even though the heat here made the action useless. At least it helped me pull my mind together.

I couldn't suggest to Ahanti that Geoff might be involved in this. Not until I talked to him at least. Surely he had a perfectly good explanation for lurking around Ahanti's apartment. Showing her this picture would only make her start fearing the person she should be able to trust the most.

I needed to talk to Geoff right away. The problem was I'd driven here with Ahanti, intending to spend at least the morning. Whether or not I could get away depended on how Mark was faring with golf. I had to admit, I wasn't sure how long a round of golf should take, but they'd been out there close to three or four hours now.

I called Mark's cell. "Hey, sweetheart. How's your morning going?"

There was something weird in his voice, almost like he was trying to prompt an answer from me without giving away which one he wanted.

That made me think he wanted an out. From what he'd told me last night, he'd never played golf before and felt the only purpose for watching it on TV was if you were having trouble sleeping. The one time my dad had taken me, I was thirteen. I got bored, wandered off to look at a turtle, and fell into a water trap. He'd never invited me again.

Hopefully Mark hadn't ended up in the water trap, too.

"Do you need a knight in shining armor?" I asked.

"That's okay. We're almost done, so if you need me, I can come."

I kept my laugh soft so it didn't carry through the phone if anyone was standing nearby. "I actually do need your help, so at least it's not a complete lie. I'm at Skin Canvas."

"I'll be there as soon as I can."

We disconnected.

I shook out my hands, trying to loosen them up. It didn't work. My fingers still felt like sausages on the ends of my palms, my engagement ring tight.

But I had to pull myself together for Ahanti. I could do that.

I ducked back inside.

Ahanti stood with her hands on her hips in front of the

teenager who'd passed me on her way in. "It doesn't matter how many times you come in. I don't give sleeves to anyone under twenty-five. Trust me, you wouldn't thank me later if I did."

I was rusty on the terminology, but I thought a *sleeve* was a tattoo that went from shoulder to wrist—a big commitment to want to make when you weren't even old enough to legally drink.

Ahanti pointed toward the door, and the girl left without an argument.

I stepped out of her path for a second time. "That sounds like a conversation you've had before."

"Too many times." Ahanti swore. "She was here that day, hanging around. I should have asked her if she saw anyone going into the back room before I shut her down."

"You didn't ask Eddie, either," Terrance piped up from behind the catalogue of gadgets he was flipping through. The front showed a red drone that looked a bit like a race car with propellers.

"Eddie wasn't here that day," Ahanti said. "Which is just my luck, since he has an excellent memory for details. He could have told us right away if Cary was here and what he did."

I would have shot Terrance a you're-not-helping glare, but he never lowered the catalogue. I squeezed Ahanti's arm. "Don't worry. Make the list, and we'll work on it methodically when I get back." I backed toward the door. "Right now, I have to go save Mark from my dad."

~

THANKFULLY, AHANTI SEEMED TO BELIEVE MY EXCUSE. IT probably helped that Mark had sounded like he needed an out. Ahanti was one of the few people who could catch me in a lie if I were truly trying to get away with it, but she knew what my dad could be like.

I called Geoff's office again and arranged to meet him for lunch. I didn't tell him why. He'd assume it was about Ahanti, and that was true enough.

Even though I'd be meeting him in a public place, I did not want to follow the pattern of so many heroines who did things that made them too stupid to live in the mystery novels I liked to read. If Geoff turned out to be the stalker, he could very well wait for me in the parking lot or slash the tires of my rental car so that I ended up on the side of the road somewhere.

No thank you. I was going to hope for the best and plan for the worst this time.

Since Geoff had never met Mark, we decided to gamble that he wouldn't know what Mark looked like. Men didn't ogle pictures of their friends the way women did. We'd failed trying to pull the trick of Mark as an innocent bystander on Ahanti, but we might get away with it on Geoff. Mark had wanted to come along upfront, but I had to have complete control over the situation to read Geoff. I couldn't mess this one up. Ahanti's future happiness—and safety—depended on it.

I picked a table with another empty one next to it and waited for Geoff. Mark took a seat at the nearby table, placing himself so that when Geoff sat, Mark would be behind him. It'd make eavesdropping easier for Mark and make Geoff less likely to notice and recognize him on the off chance he had seen a picture.

Geoff showed up almost on time. Whenever I'd had a late-morning appointment with him, he'd always been running behind. My brain logged the unusualness of it the same as it had inconsistencies in witness statements back when I'd been actively working as a lawyer.

Rearranging his schedule to arrive on time meant he wanted to be sure I didn't read in to his lateness. Poor guy didn't realize I'd also read into his promptness.

We ordered and settled in at the table.

He didn't touch his food. "How's Ahanti? She hasn't called me again since letting me know she has a stalker."

"She's managing."

I took a bite of my bacon, brie, and apricot grilled cheese. Someone really needed to open a gourmet grilled cheese place in Fair Haven. I'd go there every day.

Geoff followed my lead, though it was clear by the how-can-you-eat-at-a-time-like-this look he gave me that he was waiting for my answer and didn't want to wait long.

Based on what I knew of Geoff, he'd always seemed like a bad liar. He'd barely been able to string two coherent sentences together the week before he proposed to Ahanti. Same when he'd wanted to surprise her with the trip to the

Dominican. All of that could be an act if he were her stalker. Or it could mean that the stalking somehow fit into the delusion he'd built and so it didn't rattle him the way trying to hide a happy surprise from Ahanti did.

I wouldn't know until I pressed it. "We do have a lead on Ahanti's situation. That's why I asked you here."

He set his sandwich down and leaned forward.

I took my phone from my purse, queued up the photo of him, and handed it across the table. One of the best ways to assess someone's guilt or innocence, according to my parents, was to catch them off guard. Geoff wouldn't be expecting to see himself on my phone.

His hand twitched against his plate, pushing it away slightly. "How did you get this?"

No denying it was him. No trying to pretend it must have been taken at a different time. That was enough of an admission of some sort of guilt that I had no intention of telling him about the private investigator I'd hired. Or any other piece of information about Ahanti's safety.

"What were you doing staking out her apartment?"

He put my phone on the table, face down. He didn't want to look at it anymore, but he also wasn't reacting aggressively by shoving it back across the table to me. That spoke to shame.

Not the emotion I'd expect from her stalker. Stalkers didn't tend to exhibit shame, even when they were caught. They saw nothing wrong with their actions to be ashamed of.

"It's not what it looks like. I'm not her stalker. Or a new stalker." He took a swig of coffee that I knew must have burned all the way down—mine was still too hot to even tentatively sip.

"Has Ahanti seen these?" His words came out in a gasp, betraying him on how hot that coffee had been.

I wasn't as certain as I needed to be yet that he was innocent, but it was important that he think I believed in him. "Ahanti doesn't know about it yet. I figured there had to be some explanation, so I came to you first."

His shoulders came down, and he brought his sandwich back toward him.

As strange as it might seem to someone else, he won me over with that small change. He'd been worried about Ahanti's reaction. And I didn't think it was worry because he'd been exposed for what he was. He wasn't worried he might lose her. It seemed a lot more like worry that he'd add more stress to her when she already had enough.

"So explain it to me. Please. What were you doing there?"

"Once you told me the police couldn't get a restraining order on the guy because Ahanti didn't know who he was, I got worried. I thought if I could see someone we knew hanging around her place, it'd solve the problem." He bit into his sandwich, swallowed, and grimaced. He ran a hand over his no-doubt scalded throat. "I'm no good at it. I fell asleep."

His answer made sense. How many times had I gotten

myself into trouble because I'd wanted to help someone that the police couldn't aid? It was a good thing Mark couldn't read my thoughts, because I knew his answer would be *too many*.

Geoff and I talked for a few more minutes, mostly me assuring him that Ahanti was okay and that I was putting what resources I had behind finding her stalker. Then he headed back to work.

Once he was out of sight, Mark slipped from his table over to mine.

"Do you believe him?" he asked.

I daubed the crumbs off my plate, stalling for time. His story didn't have any holes in it that I could spot. He'd also seemed genuinely embarrassed by being caught and more concerned about Ahanti's well-being than anything else. "I can't think of any reason why he'd be stalking his fiancée or why he'd send a picture of himself with the face burned out to scare her. If he wanted to break up with her, he could have done it easier ways."

Mark leaned back in his chair. "He didn't seem like he'd want to anyway."

He hadn't. So why did I still feel all tangled up inside?

The logical side of me said it was because I'd learned to trust no one rather than because Geoff was guilty of anything worse than poor judgment. People had lied to me before, and I'd fallen for it. I'd thought people were innocent when they weren't.

If pigs flew and he turned out to be her stalker, he also

wouldn't be the first friend who I'd helped convict of a crime.

I wasn't going to gamble Ahanti's safety on my desire to be a loyal friend to Geoff.

"I'll have Rockwood Investigations look into him, maybe even tail him for a bit, just to be sure."

8

"*I*s there something wrong with my neck?" Mark asked as we headed back to the car. "My skin feels tight and like my shirt collar is rubbing against something."

I hadn't noticed anything other than a distinct sunburn starting on his face. I leaned backward. His neck was cayenne pepper-red. "You're definitely burnt."

Mark gingerly touched his fingers to the back of his neck and flinched. "That explains the headache, too. I didn't expect to get that much sun first thing in the morning." He made a face like I'd asked him to drink a whole bottle of Buckley's cough syrup. "I didn't expect to be out there for hours, either. I could have played two or three games of basketball in the same amount of time."

I tried not to laugh, but it was impossible. "We need to get you some aloe vera gel and ibuprofen."

He managed a groan, but his feet dragged. He handed me the keys. "I don't have the energy to face the traffic."

The last time I'd driven Mark rather than the other way around, he'd had a broken wrist. It killed my desire to laugh, and all my mother-hen instincts flooded to the surface. *It's just a sunburn,* I repeated over to myself.

Before meeting Mark, I hadn't realized how nerve-wracking loving someone could be. I'd have taken his sunburn onto my skin if I could have. "Were those the only reasons you faked an emergency? My dad's going to know what we were up to, by the way."

Mark shook his head, cringed, moved a hand partway to his neck, and scowled. "He says he and your mom are taking the weekend off so we can take their yacht out on Chesapeake Bay."

My hands jerked slightly, and the car veered a wheel into the other lane. A horn blared behind me, and I straightened out. Maybe I should watch the sky for pigs. If my parents were taking the weekend off, anything could happen. "They're taking the whole weekend off? You're sure?"

Mark nodded at the pace of a turtle. "You didn't mention your parents had a yacht."

He hadn't answered my question about the golfing, and the way he'd phrased his statement about the yacht was almost too careful. Something had definitely happened on that golf course. "My parents have a yacht. We never went out on it much because they could rarely manage the time away."

"I see," Mark said.

I didn't, but now didn't seem to be the time to press it.

A text came in from Ahanti a few seconds after I parked the car in the pharmacy parking lot. *Taking off early today. Too stressed to focus. Can you guys come over?*

We picked up the aloe vera, along with a tube of the strongest sunscreen we could find, and I dropped Mark off at the hotel. He'd begged off coming back with me to Ahanti's apartment, saying he needed to go sleep off his sunburn.

I didn't have the heart to tell him he'd feel worse tomorrow. I did promise to pick us up something for a late supper on my way back. When we got home, I really needed to improve my cooking skills in preparation for having a family. I didn't want my kids eating takeout every night.

Ahanti buzzed me in. She'd pushed her couch back against one wall and had pulled out the boxes where she kept her mementos.

"I'm sorting through all of it and picking out the ones I think are from the stalker."

I stepped over the circle of boxes and sat beside her, cross-legged. It was a great idea. Looking through the missives sent by the stalker would also help me prove to myself that it couldn't possibly have been Geoff. "Hopefully we can find some evidence that points to Cary."

Since so many people had already handled the mementos over the years, there wasn't any point in wearing gloves to preserve fingerprints. We started with the earliest boxes. Ahanti might be a pack rat, but she was an organized one. All her boxes of mementoes were labeled with the year, and inside were smaller boxes and folders labeled with months.

Ahanti's cheeks flushed. "Geoff teases me that it's ego keeping all this. He doesn't understand what it's like to be an artist, though. When someone hates their tattoo, or a design, or you hear someone running down tattoos in general..."

I wasn't an artist, but, on some level, I got what she meant. I'd be nice if lawyers had the same option. In a way, maybe I did in the friendships I'd made in Fair Haven by helping people. The first few months I'd been there, I'd been the town pariah, outcast because I wasn't born there and because of all the rumors circulating about me thanks to a few malicious souls. It'd taken a while, but I'd carved out a place for myself. I was now accepted as one of their own.

My engagement to a Cavanaugh hadn't hurt, either.

I got out my phone to take notes. I normally preferred working with paper and pen, but since I was living out of a hotel room, making them on my phone would keep outside eyes from seeing them, and it'd enable me to check them over whenever I needed to.

Ahanti had a pile of large freezer bags and a permanent

marker next to her. I could only imagine that she planned to package each piece of potential evidence with a date. It was that kind of organization that had made her simultaneously a successful artist and a successful business owner. Not everyone could be both.

Ahanti handed me the photo that started it all. I flipped it over. The message on the back was written in bold red marker.

"So how do we start?" Ahanti asked.

"Since this is the only thing we're certain he sent, we can use it to match the handwriting on other letters."

Ahanti shifted her gaze to the side and traced the label on the box closest to her. "It's not the only one I'm sure came from him."

It took all my courtroom training not to react. I shouldn't have been surprised. Almost everyone withheld things, embarrassed by them or thinking they weren't important. I'd just figured Ahanti would know better after all her years of friendship with me. "Show me the others."

She scrounged through the box marked APRIL and handed me two cards. The contents weren't X-rated, but they were definitely more intimate than what a normal customer would have written, mentioning the softness of her touch and the smell of her hair when she leaned over him.

The notes were handwritten, with no more grammatical errors than I would have expected from anyone. That left us without a clue to the sender's intelligence or education level.

I snapped pictures of both the notes and the photo of Geoff, front and back. The cards were in black pen instead of the red marker on the photo, so the letters were fatter on the picture and the writing blockier and less clear. The handwriting looked like it might be the same, though it was a little hard to tell.

Ahanti was watching me as if she expected a lecture. She kind of deserved one for not telling anyone how far the letter writer had gone before now. Lecturing her wouldn't change anything, though. "Well, at least we have a bigger sample size."

I tugged the May box toward me while Ahanti took the June one. She didn't remember him sending anything in either of those months other than the picture of Geoff, but we had to be thorough. It seemed strange that the stalker would skip such a long stretch of time.

I crossed my mental fingers. Combing through evidence could be a slow process. We wouldn't have any answers in the hour-length of a TV show. Real evidence collection was like going on a scavenger hunt or following a trail of footprints and broken branches through the woods.

Ahanti was right about May. I didn't find anything that matched or had a similar tone. Most of the cards and notes were simple thank-yous. A few looked like they'd been originally attached to a gift like a bottle of wine.

"You get a lot of appreciative clients."

Ahanti shrugged. "I only do custom work, so we spend a lot of time together. I've also got a reputation for being able to fix old tattoos or botched jobs and turn them into something beautiful that looks like they intended it that way all along. I've even had a few chemo patients whose eyebrows never grew back in coming for cosmetic help. Those ones I do at cost." She lovingly stroked the card in her hand. "This one was from a woman who had a nasty scar on her arm from a car accident. She'd given up wearing t-shirts or a bathing suit because she couldn't stand the stares. We hid it under a gorgeous rose as part of the stem. That was a good day."

Ahanti and Terrance were the only tattoo artists I knew, but it seemed like, while they were giving people tattoos, they were often also giving them so much more.

I moved back to the February box. Nothing there, either. Ahanti also came up empty with January.

I tapped a card against the box edge. The gaps really bothered me. Why only send her things in some months and not others? If Cary were her stalker, shouldn't he have shown some consistency?

I popped the lid on November's box. Ahanti was already halfway into December's.

She sucked in a breath and passed the card in her hand over to me. The handwriting seemed to match. This one talked about what a gift she was to him. I took a picture.

She gave a visible shiver. "The worst part is he keeps

repeating the gift idea." She flipped the card over so I could see the front had a sparkly gift box on it. "I think he knows my name means *gift*."

I'd missed that connection completely. The police likely would have, too, if they'd been presented with it. It was a very personal thing. "Do you remember if anyone asked you the meaning of your name?"

She held the card pinched between two fingers like it was filthy and dropped it into a freezer bag. "Only Terrance. Back at Cary's, when we'd been working together a few months." She shot me a look like she could guess what I'd say in response. "But this isn't Terrance. Cary was there too. He would have heard it."

It was almost 8:00 by the time we finished. Even with the gaps, there'd been a disturbing number of messages with similar handwriting and tone.

I'd texted with Mark a couple of times during the process, and he'd told me to take as long as I needed to finish. He blamed his sunburn for also destroying his appetite. He was considering raiding the hotel ice machine to create an ice pack.

Ahanti carried boxes back to their stack while I finished the one belonging to the month she'd left Cary's studio to start Skin Canvas.

I was down to only two items left in the box. It looked like he might not have written her that month. According to Ahanti, there hadn't been any message prior to her leaving Cary's studio, either. That would make sense if her stalker were Cary. He wouldn't have been stalking her prior to their romantic and business break-up.

The second last letter was from a woman. She'd signed her name.

The final card wasn't signed. And the handwriting seemed to match. I might have found the first one he'd ever sent. It'd been eerie working back through the messages and seeing his progression in reverse. This note could give us a clue to when he moved from interest to obsession with Ahanti.

It didn't automatically cross Cary off the list because it'd been sent during a month when she was still at his studio part of the time. He could have sent it after she left. We'd have our trigger. We'd know it was Cary.

The note was a short one—congratulating Ahanti on the change she'd made.

My lungs felt like they shrunk down to half capacity. Cary wouldn't have congratulated her on leaving him.

When Ahanti had her back turned, I snapped a photo of the card and tucked it into the freezer bag. Hopefully she wouldn't want to see it and dig it out.

"I found one from right after you stopped working with Cary." I kept my voice casual. Controlling my intonation would probably never be easy, but it seemed like my mom had been right that, the more I practiced, the better I got. Whether improving my ability to deceive was a good thing or a bad one was a matter of perspective. "At least we know when it started."

She yawned and didn't ask what was in the note. Since I hadn't specifically mentioned it, she probably assumed it was identical to the rest. Until I could talk this over with Mark, I needed to let her think that.

Because if Cary turned out not to be her stalker, we had a much bigger problem.

The man in all these notes knew her well. He was determined.

And he was most likely one of the two men she was closest to—Geoff or Terrance.

Over our takeout dinner, I caught Mark up on the notes I'd taken and showed him the picture of the first missive. It seemed like a good thing that Mark had stayed behind. He could barely move without wincing. His arms were as red as his neck.

As soon as I finished eating, I grabbed the tube of aloe vera and made him sit on the edge of the bed.

"That first note is innocent enough," Mark said. "But you're right. Unless your PI finds something solid to show Cary's her stalker, I don't think it's him. Besides, if he was trying to use the card to make nice, he would have signed his name."

I squirted a dollop of gel onto my fingers. "Maybe he assumed she'd recognize his writing."

I touched my fingers to Mark's skin. He gasped and

recoiled.

How badly burned was he? He was a doctor, so he should know if it was bad enough to go to an ER, but he did always say he had more experience with dead people than with live ones as a medical examiner. "Should we have gotten this looked at?"

He stuck his arm back out. "It's just cold." He inclined his head toward where my phone rested on the bed, the picture of the first note still on the screen. "Would you recognize my handwriting?"

Yes jumped to my lips but stuck there. Mark and I texted and emailed and called each other, none of which involved writing by hand. I'd never even seen his handwriting, and we were engaged.

His lifted his shoulders a touch. "Because I wouldn't recognize yours. People don't write much out by hand anymore. Even most appointments are entered into computers or phones, and reminders are sent by text and email."

It explained how this looked like someone Ahanti knew well and yet she didn't recognize their handwriting at all.

I finished Mark's first arm and moved on to the second one in silence. The thought that this might be someone other than Cary made my back and shoulders ache like I'd been trying to haul the sleigh my Clydesdale horses pulled in the winter back home.

My fingers stalled near his elbow. "Did you think Geoff

was telling the truth about why he was outside Ahanti's apartment?"

If my hand hadn't been on his arm, I wouldn't have felt his muscles tense, the movement was so subtle. "I don't know him well, but it's something I would have done."

It was something he'd done on a smaller level. Back when I'd thought he was married and I told him I couldn't be around him anymore, he'd still sat outside the animal shelter until Russ arrived to make sure a murderer didn't catch me there alone.

"You introduced them, didn't you?" Mark asked. "So Geoff didn't even know her back when she was working with Cary."

As far as I knew, I'd introduced them that night we accidentally bumped into him at the movies.

I wished I could shut off the part of my brain trained by my parents to think up all the alternative explanations. Like that he'd only pretended to bump into us there. Like that he'd actually followed her there, hoping I'd introduce them and ask him to sit with us, which is exactly what I did.

"I started going to Geoff as my chiropractor because we always seemed to be standing in line at the same time at the Starbucks right down the street from Ahanti and my apartment building. I'd never been to a chiropractor before, but I'd been in pain since I fell off my bike."

I crawled up onto the bed behind Mark so that I could work on his neck, but I kept my hands on his shoulders for a second instead. I wanted to hear his reaction.

"Was his office near there?" His voice was a little too measured.

His current offices weren't, nor was his apartment. "At the time he said they were but that he was in the process of changing locations...I never saw the old office that he claimed was nearby."

"Have you asked the private investigator to look into Geoff as well?"

I hadn't yet. I'd intended to after our lunch meeting, but then the text from Ahanti drove it from my mind. "I'll call him first thing tomorrow."

"We'd still have to explain why he'd have sent Ahanti a picture of him with his own face burnt out, though. Even if we could establish that he might have seen her somewhere, become obsessed, and then been looking for an introduction, that photo doesn't fit."

The only thing I could think of was that Geoff was getting jealous of how much of Ahanti's attention was going elsewhere, onto her clients, onto wedding plans, onto hunting for a new apartment. "Maybe he thought she was too focused on other things. If someone threatened him, it would bring them closer together. But it backfired on him."

I gently applied the aloe vera to the back of Mark's neck. Along with talking to the PI, I'd also have to find a way to subtly ask Ahanti how the wedding plans were going prior to this and how Geoff was handling all the stress.

Mark snagged my hand with his, stopping my progress on his neck. "Might be time for you to go back to your room, or I'm going to want you to stay."

The lines we'd drawn in our relationship were getting harder and harder to maintain the longer we were together and the closer we got to our wedding. Sticking to what we believed meant that we had to respect when the other person was tempted to cross those lines. I'd been thinking about sunburns and stalkers, but apparently, my ministrations had taken Mark's mind somewhere else.

I capped the aloe vera gel, handed it to him, and kissed him gently on the cheek. "I'll see you in the morning."

When this was all over, I'd turn my attention to planning a honeymoon for Mark and me in whatever country had the lowest murder rate.

9

*M*ark settled in beside me on the bow of my parents' yacht. His sunburn had faded some after two days, and now he complained about it itching more than hurting. We'd made sure to pack extra sunscreen and a hat before we left yesterday for the weekend trip.

My parents had actually taken a weekend off to spend it with us on the Chesapeake. It was a minor miracle.

Mark smiled big enough that his dimples came out in full force, warming me more than the summer sun did. "You had a rough childhood, didn't you?"

My return laugh stuck in my throat. At one time, I'd thought I had. My parents had been always working and were emotionally unavailable when they were home. I'd always felt the pressure of living up to their seemingly unreachable expectations.

Now that I had seen more of life outside of the wealthy DC area and the equally wealthy vacation spots we'd been to, I had a new appreciation for how easy my life had been. I could have easily turned out spoiled and entitled had my parents not emphasized the value of hard work and responsibility, and had my Uncle Stan not taken the time to show me that even those were worthless if you didn't also have compassion.

I leaned my face back and let the breeze ruffle through my hair. I'd almost forgotten how much I loved being on the water. Despite owning this boat, my parents rarely had time to use it.

"Maybe we should have a boat someday. Not one this size, obviously, but I'd like to be able to take our kids out onto the lake on weekends."

I glanced over at Mark, but both his dimples and smile were gone. There was a tenseness to his jaw that sent a chill over me from the inside out.

He took my hand and ran his thumb over my knuckles. "Is what you were raised with the kind of life you want?"

"Why are you asking that?"

He glanced up at the fly bridge where my dad captained the boat. "Turned out it wasn't just your dad and me golfing on Thursday. He'd also invited DC's chief medical examiner and the head of Howard University Hospital's pathology department."

Little black spots burst in my vision like I'd been staring at reflections off the water too long. I closed my eyes, but they only turned into colored opposites. I forced them open again. "He made you an offer. My dad."

Mark nodded. "He said he wanted me to see the kind of connections he has so I'd know that I could take my career in whatever direction I wanted if I chose not to take the toxicology research position. He'd make sure I got whatever job I wanted in the area."

The choice words that swam to the front of my mind were ones I rarely contemplated saying. None of them, as my grandmother would have said, were fit for a lady.

Mark's grip tightened on my hand. "He also said that one day you'd regret leaving DC and the type of life you could have had here if you worked at their firm as a partner."

That was the first I'd ever heard about me becoming a partner in their firm. Theoretically, that's what they'd always intended, but I'd assumed that when they saw how inept I was in front of a jury, they'd changed their plans. Either way, it was another case of my parents planning my future without ever consulting me.

I didn't blame Mark for wondering if what my dad said about me was true. Mark had known me for less than a year. My dad had known me my whole life. It'd be natural for Mark to wonder if my dad knew me better.

My dad could get into people's heads and twist their minds around until they believed everything he told them. His forceful personality, logical-sounding arguments, and charisma worked on people in his everyday life just as much as they worked on jury members when he wanted them to.

This had to stop. My dad wasn't a man who understood the word *no*, but it was time he learned. "It sounds like my dad and i need to have a talk."

I tried to stand but only made it to my knees. Mark kept hold of my hand. "Not today. Your mom took today off of work the same as your dad, and I think she's enjoying having you back."

I slumped back to the deck. As much as I wanted to toss my dad over the side into the Chesapeake, my mom hadn't been to blame this time. When she suggested Mark for the research position, she'd given us an option, and she hadn't bribed and blackmailed like my dad. It wouldn't be right to ruin this day for her. It took a lot to get her away from work, even on a Saturday, and I had to believe she'd done it out of love for me.

My phone vibrated in my pocket, jerking me out of my mulling. I twitched. I'd gotten used to all the dead zones in Fair Haven. I hadn't expected to get cell phone reception out here.

My caller display flashed a picture of Ahanti. That was weird. She knew we were out on the water today, and she should be at work trying to catch up on the clients she'd had to reschedule earlier this week.

My mouth went dry. The only reason I could think of for her to be calling me was that her stalker had done something new.

I tapped the answer icon.

"Nicole?" her voice wobbled. "It wasn't Cary."

Crap. Sometimes it wasn't nice to be right. "What happened?"

"I'm at the police station."

Too many questions ran through my mind to pick one. Had he left something disturbing enough that she'd felt the need to take it in immediately? How did she know it hadn't come from Cary? Why had she gone to the station rather than calling the police to come to her?

She sounded more frazzled than would result from another card.

"Why are you at the police station? Are you okay?"

"Geoff's here too. They wouldn't let me talk to him."

Double crap. I did not like the direction this was headed.

I glanced back. The bow of the boat wasn't technically set up for passengers to ride on. I'd just always liked it, and it was flat enough to be safe. But getting up here required a narrow path and two hands to hold the railing. I couldn't make it back to the actual deck with one hand without risking dumping myself into the water. If I went overboard, it'd only delay our return even more.

Please ask my dad to turn around, I mouthed to Mark.

My dad wouldn't normally change his plans, but I was wagering he'd be very accommodating to Mark right now, given that he wanted to woo him to the dark side.

I shifted my phone to the other ear. "Ahanti, I need you to start over. I don't understand what's going on."

"Cary's dead."

For the second time today, I thought about using a word stronger than *crap*. There was only one reason the police would have brought both Ahanti and Geoff down to the station for that.

They thought one of them had killed him.

10

By the time my dad docked the boat and we made the almost four-hour drive from Hampton Roads back to the city, it was well past supper—a fact my dad had been sure to point out to me, along with how the police would have given them both a meal and then collected their trash to take a sneaky DNA sample.

I'd told him that neither Ahanti nor Geoff had killed Cary and so it wouldn't matter.

The look he'd given me had clearly said I was too naïve and needed to stop trusting people so much.

For my mom's sake, I kept my response to myself. One thing I wasn't was naïve. No one could see as many bodies as I had in the past year and remain naïve. But, to my dad, trusting anyone other than your spouse—and sometimes even trusting them—made a person naïve.

Sufficed to say, the drive back was a quiet one except

for the stilted conversation my mom and Mark attempted for the first hour.

Halfway there, I got a text from Mandy, asking if she should throw the nylon leashes out. They were a menace and a danger. They could probably saw wood. My response that they weren't a menace where I'd left them behind my dog food bag might have been a little harsher than the situation warranted. I had a niggling suspicion they'd be gone by the time I got home anyway.

When my dad stopped the car in front of the hotel, my mom swiveled in her seat to face me in the back. "I have an outfit in the trunk that I picked up from the dry cleaners yesterday. Did you want me to join you?"

The muscles in my whole upper body tensed like she'd thrown something at me.

She's not saying you're incapable, the little voice of reason in my head said. *She's offering because there's two of them and one of you.*

"Yes, please."

My dad said nothing, not even goodbye, as we got out of the car, but the self-satisfied smile on his face made me want to kick his tires.

He thought this proved him right. About me. About everything. He thought he'd won.

~

It was another forty-five minutes before my mom and I were dressed and to the police station in our rental car.

As much as I hated my dad's smug attitude, I had to admit that I liked the new dynamic that my mom and I had developed while she was in Fair Haven. I'd thought it might have been an isolated situation, given that we were working for the police rather than against them, but I felt it here again. She treated me more as an equal and less as an inept protégée. During the ride, I briefed her on the situation.

As soon as we reached the station, an officer showed me into the interview room where Ahanti waited.

A half-empty water bottle sat on the table next to her, and she'd used the pad of paper and pen they'd left her to doodle intricate designs that looked a bit like those mandalas in the adult coloring books that everyone was so crazy about a couple of years ago. Some of her mascara had rubbed off onto the underside of her eyes, making her look even more tired and sad than she probably was.

Despite everything that had gone on between her and Cary, despite the suspicion that he might have been stalking her and might have threatened Geoff, I could almost see her thinking about the good times they'd had. He had helped her get her start. She had cared about him once.

"My mom's with Geoff." I pulled out the chair next to her and sat. "So you don't have to worry about him."

She rested her forehead in her hands for a couple of

beats. "That's good. I got the idea they think we planned it together, but that he carried it out." Her voice carried a this-can't-be-happening tone.

I scooted the chair in closer. My mom and I would get this straightened out as soon as possible. "What have they said to you so far?"

She pulled the pad of paper closer to her and picked at the edge. "Not much. Someone stabbed Cary last night when he was closing up his studio. I tried to explain to them that we thought Cary had been stalking me. I meant it to show that he was a danger to me, not the other way around, but they took it as motive. The detective said something about Cary and me having a prior relationship that ended badly. That's when I asked to call my lawyer."

She'd done the right thing, but the timing would have made the detective more suspicious than he already was.

While I knew Ahanti well enough to know that she wouldn't have turned the tables on Cary by killing him, I did have to ask a question she wasn't going to like. "How confident are you that Geoff wasn't involved in this?"

She picked at the paper so hard the corner ripped off. "Ninety-nine percent."

"Why only ninety-nine?"

"You can't be one hundred percent certain about anything in life."

Classic Ahanti grayscale, but if we couldn't get this situation cleared up soon, we'd have to talk about her fudging her life philosophies a little when the police talked to her again.

The detective who came through the door looked young enough that this might have been his first case after being promoted. That they sent us a relatively inexperienced detective was a good sign. Besides, unless he was a prodigy, I could handle him. Better my mom be with Geoff. If they thought he'd been the one to carry out the crime, they'd lean heavier on him.

"I assume you've had enough time to confer with your lawyer," the detective said.

I didn't miss the slight that he failed to introduce himself to me. That meant he might already know who I was. If he did, my last name alone would put him on high alert. Fitzhenry-Dawes had a reputation for defending people who were guilty.

I'd go with a hackneyed response and hope it made him underestimate me. "We've had plenty of time, since my client had nothing to do with this."

His slight eyebrow raise said *trite*. Which I marked as a win for me.

He pulled the pad of paper back toward him from where it sat in front of Ahanti. He glanced at it, and I couldn't be sure, but I'd have sworn he rolled his eyes. He tore the top page off to reveal the blank one underneath.

"I don't suppose your client can provide an alibi to substantiate that claim."

Ahanti said Cary died when he was closing up his

studio. It wasn't unusual for Skin Canvas to stay open until almost midnight. If Cary stayed open as late, I knew Ahanti was home alone, which sounded like yet another cliché. Cary also wasn't as busy as Skin Canvas, though.

"What's the time of death window?"

"Between 6:00 and 8:00 last night."

I shut down both a smile and a cringe. She had an alibi, and when the detective heard it, he'd be convinced I was lying. "She was with me during that time."

This time he openly rolled his eyes. "Convenient that she was meeting with her lawyer at the same time as her former boyfriend was murdered. Almost like she knew she'd need an alibi." The mocking drained out of his tone and the look he gave Ahanti could have left a bruise. "But as I'm sure your attorney told you, conspiracy to commit murder is punishable with the same sentence as committing the act yourself."

Ahanti maintained her composure. She didn't shoot a look in my direction. She didn't give any indication of what she was thinking.

I'd been expecting her to react. *Maybe she already knew,* the tiny, always-suspicious voice in my head whispered. *Maybe she and Geoff* did *plan this together.*

"It wouldn't make sense for us to kill Cary," Ahanti said. "We weren't even sure he was stalking me."

Then I saw it in the way she held extra still. I-don't-know-what-to-do Ahanti was frantic, like a squirrel who can't decide which direction to run from the cars bearing down on them. That's the Ahanti I'd been expecting. This was business Ahanti, the one who might screw up a part of a tattoo but always knew she could fix it. She knew she hadn't been a part of anything illegal, and so she trusted that this could be fixed. That's why she was so calm despite her nerves.

I really did need a vacation when I started suspecting my best friend was capable of murder. The next thing I knew, I'd be doubting Mark, too.

The detective leaned back in his chair as if he thought Ahanti's reaction was too calm as well. "Maybe you and your new boyfriend didn't want to take the chance."

The same look flared in Ahanti's eyes as when she wanted to tattoo *cheater* on my ex-boyfriend's forehead. "Geoff's a chiropractor. If he wanted to kill Cary, he wouldn't have stabbed him. He would have snuck up behind him and broken his neck. Geoff's so squeamish about blood he can barely stand to be in my studio, and he's lucky not to take off a finger with his dinner knife. He'd never stab someone."

She certainly sounded more than ninety-nine percent certain of his innocence. Some of that was likely her protective instincts because she felt Geoff was threatened, but helped ease some of my lingering concern that Geoff might have killed Cary on his own.

The detective must have sensed the sincerity of Ahanti's response, too, which raised my estimation of him a little. He got to his feet and went to the door.

"Don't plan any trips out of town anytime soon. If it looks like your fiancé did it, we're going to have more questions for you." He held the door open like he expected us to leave. "And if you want to look less guilty, you might want to choose a different law firm."

The detective's foot was close enough I could have stomped it on my way by and pretended it was an accident. Ahanti was innocent, and I wasn't my parents. Instead I gave him my sweetest smile as if he'd paid me a compliment.

Know where you're weak, my dad used to tell me, *and where they might be able to hurt you. Then turn it around and use it as a weapon against them.*

I paused outside the door and looked back at the detective over my shoulder. "Our firm does handle cases for clients who aren't innocent, but that means we're the perfect choice for someone who is. Defending an innocent person will be easy by comparison."

Ahanti looked like she wanted to high-five me. I decided not to tell her what I'd said wasn't exactly true. Sometimes defending an innocent person could be as hard as defending a guilty one.

We headed straight for the parking lot, and I walked with Ahanti to her car.

She hit her clicker to unlock it, but paused with her hand on the door handle. All the confidence and bravado was gone from her face. For a breath, I was afraid she was going to ask me if I thought Geoff had something to do with it after all, and I would have had to admit that I wasn't sure. If Geoff was the one actually stalking her, Cary would be a perfect scapegoat for his anger at being separated from Ahanti. Plus, he'd have had every reason to believe that, if Cary—her perceived stalker—died, things with Ahanti would return to the way they had been.

"I was never good at math," Ahanti said. "It's one of the reasons I dropped out of pre-med. But the odds seem obvious here even to me. It's not likely Cary's death was random, is it?"

I shook my head.

She fingered her keys and gave a sharp nod. "I was hoping I was wrong and there was some explanation where he was my stalker after all."

Not unless he was also stalking someone else and that person, or someone connected to them, killed him. The likelihood of him being her stalker now seemed impossibly slim, especially given that the original note from her stalker had already made me think Cary wasn't the one. "Probably not."

Ahanti swore. And not softly, either. "Could you ride back to my apartment with me? Eddie hasn't had a chance to check my security system and locks yet."

I understood what she didn't say. We'd been looking at the wrong person, and she didn't feel safe going back to an empty apartment alone in case the real stalker found a way in and was waiting for her. "I'll came and stay with you until my mom's done here."

I texted my mom and Mark to let them know what I was doing.

Going back with her would also give us an opportunity to brainstorm other possibilities for her stalker. Hopefully Ahanti could come up with better suggestions that the ones that were swimming around in my mind. The only two potential suspects I had at present were Geoff and Terrance.

I climbed in and buckled up. We'd already looked at the content of the messages. There didn't seem to be much more we could get from them about the stalker's identity. We'd have to come at this from a different direction.

When we'd thought it was Cary, we'd planned to ask anyone who was in Skin Canvas the day the picture of Geoff was dropped off if they'd seen him. Now the list Ahanti was supposed to make would have added meaning. The people on it were either potential witnesses or our stalker.

he list Ahanti dropped into my lap as I sat on her couch was much longer than expected. I'd thought she'd have five, maybe six, people on the list. I hadn't counted the names, but it looked to be at least twenty. "How many hours did you work that day?"

Ahanti shrugged. "We didn't close until close to midnight. Terrance and I both stayed the whole time."

Well, twenty was still better than the times I'd basically had an entire town full of suspects. The only name I recognized was Terrance's. "You're going to have to run down this list and tell me who all these people are."

Not everyone on the list was a client. Three quarters of them were, between Ahanti and Terrance. Apparently, that Wednesday, Ahanti had booked a lot of design consults rather than actually tattooing, which meant she'd seen more people than usual. She'd also included the name of the mailman who dropped off their mail—"Because I can't be sure he didn't leave the picture in an unmarked envelope along with the actual mail"—a supplier who was trying to get her to switch to a new brand of ink—"But I don't think it was him because that's the first time he'd been in"—and the girl who kept coming back even though Ahanti refused to tattoo her. I was personally pretty sure that refusing to give someone a tattoo wasn't grounds for stalking. Besides, Ahanti said she'd only been hanging around the last few weeks.

I drew a line through the supplier's name. Since Ahanti hadn't ever seen him before, he wasn't our guy, and he also wouldn't be much help in figuring out who might have gone into the back room.

Through the back of the paper, under the names written on it, I could see the preliminary sketches Ahanti must have done back during the design process for her engagement ring. Geoff knew she'd never be happy with something someone else created, so they'd waited for her to create her own and have it custom made. It seemed almost sacrilege to even consider that same man would be her stalker. His name wasn't on the list.

But my parents had trained me that we couldn't allow how we felt about a witness to change our questions or make us let them off easy. Doing so could destroy our client's case. In this situation, it could cost Ahanti her life. "Did Geoff come by that day?"

I kept my gaze focused on the list and tried to keep my

tone light. Ahanti and I had never had a fight over a guy, though she hadn't liked Peter when I'd been dating him. I didn't want to start a fight now. Her instinct was to defend Geoff.

"Why?" she asked, equally as casually.

So casually, in fact, that I couldn't tell if she suspected anything. Even if she did, the fact that she didn't want to let on to me said she didn't take my possible suspicion of Geoff seriously. I'd already asked her if he might have killed Cary. She must realize that, as a lawyer, I had to ask some questions whether I wanted to or not.

Still, I wasn't ready to even hint that Geoff might be somehow involved with this whole situation. "Everyone who was there is a witness."

Ahanti dropped onto the couch next to me. "He brought me supper that night. He knew I'd be working late."

That might actually clear him, depending on when Ahanti discovered the photo. "And when did you check the mail and other stuff on your desk."

Her eyebrows lowered slightly. "Why does that matter?"

Be careful, Nikki. "If you'd already found the picture by then, we don't need to bother Geoff by asking him a lot of questions. He probably has enough on his mind after the police interrogation."

My mom hadn't texted or called yet, which meant the police hadn't released Geoff. They were certainly spending more time on him than on Ahanti.

"I didn't notice it until right before I closed the studio." Her fingers drew lines on her thighs as if itching to pick up a pencil and draw to relieve some stress. "Do you think Cary's murder is linked to my stalker somehow?"

Mark's favorite phrase of *possible but not probable* came to mind. Though how much more likely was it that Cary would be killed at the same time as Ahanti was being stalked? It wasn't like they were part of a gang where multiple people who knew each other could be hurt in unrelated events. It might actually be probable as well as possible.

My heart beat a few slow, sickening thuds. If the two cases were related, then either Geoff had killed Cary to protect Ahanti or her stalker had somehow felt eliminating Cary was in his best interest. The two might even intersect if Geoff was her stalker.

If he wasn't, then the real stalker was now systematically targeting people close to Ahanti. First they'd threatened Geoff, her fiancé. Now they'd killed Cary, her former boss and boyfriend.

Her separation from Geoff might have actually saved his life, but everyone else she was close to was in danger—including me. Mark was going to *love* that.

Ahanti's hands clenched over her knees. "That was too long a pause. You do think the two things are connected."

Stupid me. "It's something we need to consider, but it could also have been a random mugging. It's not a stretch that someone might have thought Cary would have cash on hand." I squeezed her hand. "Besides, if it is connected, at least it means the police will be investigating, too. When they catch this guy, they'll be able to send him to prison, where he can't harm you or anyone else again."

And I'd make sure that even if the guy had money for it, he wouldn't be represented by Fitzhenry-Dawes.

I smoothed the list of names on my lap. "Right now, the best thing we can do is try to figure out who might have left that photo. Then we can pass that information along to the police."

Ahanti finally squeezed my hand in return. "Since the letters have been coming a long time, we can cross off recent clients."

She reached for the pen.

I blocked her hand. "Not necessarily. It's not unusual for stalkers to watch for a long time before making contact." I pulled out my phone and checked the notes I made when we were looking at the messages. I'd been able to put together a bit of a timeline. "I think we can safely assume that your stalker's been a client for at least two years, though. That's when he first mentions something about how gentle you are, so you must have had contact by then."

"But it could have been earlier?"

I nodded.

She took the pen, her tongue peeking out from between her teeth. "That also means Terrance's clients might have seen something, but can't be my stalker."

She added X marks by a few more names.

"Have you ever touched your mailman?" I asked.

She put an X beside him as well. Terrance's name was written right above.

Ahanti hadn't loved me hinting at Terrance as her stalker any more than she'd liked me suggesting Geoff had something to do with it. But Terrance knew her name meant *gift*. Most of the other people on this list wouldn't, unless they'd wondered about it and searched on the Internet. That seemed like a stretch. He'd deliberately used the gift motif, which he wasn't likely to do unless he'd heard it from Ahanti and felt the meaning of her name was important to her.

"How about Terrance?" I tried to make it sound like I was simply crossing off the least likely people first.

"It's not Terrance," Ahanti said and put an X beside his name.

But she hadn't answered my question, and Terrance had tattoos up both his arms. "Are you the one who does Terrance's tattoos?"

"We trade services," she said. Her words sounded pinched, like she was clenching her jaw. "But Terrance has known I was dating Geoff from the start. He wouldn't have suddenly decided to send a picture with Geoff's face burnt out now."

That was another part we still needed to explain if we wanted to be able to pinpoint her stalker. The stalker might have killed Cary because he perceived him as a threat to Ahanti. Or he might have seen him as a competitor for her attention. But why threaten Geoff now? Why not when they started apartment hunting? Why not months ago when they got engaged? Why not back when they started dating, for that matter?

"Can you think of anything that's changed between you and Geoff recently that might have caused the stalker to escalate? Did you have a public fight?"

That would have been ideal since it would narrow our suspect list to people who were around for both the fight and the day the photo was delivered.

Ahanti snagged a piece of paper from the side table, flipped it over, and doodled on it without paying much attention. "Not a chance. You know Geoff. He'd rather concede than fight in public and make any sort of a scene."

She continued to draw, and her engagement ring caught the light. They'd been engaged months ago, but...I flipped the paper on my lap over.

The sketches bore only a few similarities to her final design, kept around now for scrap. The design had taken her months and, in that time, she hadn't worn a ring. She'd texted me a picture of it on her hand when it'd finally been finished.

I switched to my text messages and scrolled back. That was only three weeks ago.

My theory only worked, though, if she and Geoff had done something similar to Mark and me and kept their engagement mostly private until she had the ring. I'd known about it, and they'd begun making arrangements, but they might not have told everyone. Without a ring, it wouldn't have been obvious, and I knew Ahanti hadn't posted it on social media until she had the ring to flaunt.

"I think it might have been your ring. How many people knew about the engagement before your ring was finished?"

Her pen slipped from her fingers and rolled onto the couch. "Almost no one knew. Just you and our families."

We had our trigger.

My phone beeped, and I glanced at the text in case it was my mom. It was.

I held my phone out to show Ahanti the sender. "They're releasing Geoff for now. My mom wants to know if you feel up to bringing me back to the hotel. She wants to see the material from the stalker and ask you a few questions. She suspects the two cases are related."

Ahanti nodded. "Let me grab a sweater and pull on some jeans. Hotel air conditioning is always too cold."

I took a picture of the list of names as a back-up while I waited. It was another lawyerly trait that I couldn't seem to shake.

I didn't know what my future held in terms of practicing law, but based on what Mark had told me earlier today, my dad and I needed to have a talk. Whatever decision I made—

Ahanti screamed.

12

I jumped to my feet and spun around, but then my legs felt stiff, like someone had dunked my bottom half in liquid nitrogen.

Ahanti stared down at something on the top of her dresser, her hand pressed to her mouth and a sweater and pair of jeans crumpled on the floor at her feet.

She sprinted toward the bathroom.

My brain and my legs came back to life at the same time. The walk across the studio apartment felt abnormally long, like I'd stepped into some sort of carnival funhouse.

As I passed the bathroom, Ahanti sat on the floor, slumped over the toilet. I didn't stop.

Before I could comfort her, before I could decide what to do, I had to see what was on that dresser. The closer I got, the more I wanted to turn back. To take Ahanti and leave the apartment and hide somewhere and pretend like she didn't have a stalker and I hadn't already seen too many horrible things to ever feel safe again.

A knife rested on the dresser. Dried rust red stained the blade.

Heat burned through my stomach and up into my throat. I almost turned back to join Ahanti in the bathroom. But I couldn't. I had to see it, and then I had to call the police.

One step closer and I could make out the paper lying beneath the knife like it was a macabre paperweight.

On the paper was a printout of a picture of Cary lying on the ground. He was dead. Below it, someone had scrawled a message.

Sorry I missed you. I took care of the problem. I'll always take care of you. See you soon.

I sank down onto the edge of the bed. Ahanti came out of the bathroom, wiping her mouth with a washcloth. She looked stunned, almost numb.

I turned her around and led her back to the bathroom. "I'm calling the police. Get what you absolutely need. You won't be able to stay here tonight."

I dialed 911, and for the first time, I wished the officers who were going to respond would include Fair Haven's Chief McTavish. He and I might be like anchovies and chocolate together, but I knew how he worked and how he'd treat a case like this. In DC, even though this was a homicide now, it likely still wouldn't be a priority.

I gave the dispatcher the name of the detective we'd

originally spoken to about Ahanti's stalker and had Ahanti provide the name of the detective who interviewed her earlier today. Then I texted my mom and Mark, and snapped a picture of the knife and message as well. The police doubtless wouldn't like that if they found out, but I knew my mom would approve.

Detective DeGoey—as Ahanti had informed me his name was—arrived on the scene with the responding officers. A small part of me wondered what it said about me that, in my mind, my best friend's home had become "the scene." Did it mean my parents were right about my inability to completely give up the law? I shoved the idea to the back of my mind. It could wait.

DeGoey and the officers went over to where the knife sat and talked quietly. He called someone on his cell phone and came back over to where I stood. I'd decided to follow my dad's lead and not sit. That way I wouldn't have to look up at DeGoey like a naughty child.

DeGoey came back across the apartment and stopped next to me. He gave me a look I couldn't interpret. "For an innocent woman, she spends a lot of time with her lawyer."

What I wanted to do was snub him, but that would be counterproductive. He wasn't the detective trying to prove Ahanti had committed a murder anymore. He was the detective who was trying to solve Cary's murder, a murder we now knew intersected with Ahanti's stalker. Hopefully he'd understand that distinction soon. As much as it galled me, that meant we'd be better off with him as an ally.

I gave him a smile so sweet it practically dripped honey. "Most people don't have a defense attorney for a friend. That's the capacity I was here as when we discovered the knife and the note, and that's why I was here Thursday night as well."

His eyebrows were too thin for a man's. They flattened a bit now and almost disappeared. "You also didn't mention before that you weren't some underling from Fitzhenry-Dawes. You *are* a Fitzhenry-Dawes."

His barriers were going to be harder to crack than the Fair Haven officers'. Good thing I wasn't a quitter. "Would it have mattered if I did?"

His lips curved into the world's tiniest smile. "Not in a positive way." He motioned back toward the two officers. "We'll have to close this place up to fingerprint it. I hope for her sake"—he looked over my shoulder, I assumed at Ahanti—"that we find some because the timing is almost too convenient. She comes home from being questioned by the police about her ex-boyfriend's murder, and the real murderer has left a confession in her apartment."

I could have protested that I'd gone back here with her right afterward, but that wouldn't help. He could easily suggest she'd left it here before, just in case. And while I doubted he'd ever say it out loud, he clearly didn't think well of my parents' firm. He might even think I'd helped her create this situation so there'd be reasonable doubt for a jury.

Besides, any of that obscured the real solution here. I

definitely hadn't accrued enough goodwill for him to follow it for my sake, but maybe he'd listen to reason. When we took away all the layers, he and I both wanted the same thing—to catch the person responsible. "We've already been to the police because she has a stalker. We believed that stalker might be the deceased, but now it seems her stalker is your murderer. We have the messages her stalker sent her. I think you'll find the handwriting is a match. I'm hoping you'll be willing to look into it as an option."

He stone-faced me but said, "Show me."

Thankfully, we'd already separated out the stalker's messages from Ahanti's other fan mail. I brought him over to the box and waited nearby while he glanced through it.

Finally, he straightened. "I'll take it with me for handwriting analysis and to check for matching prints. The handwriting looks similar, but that doesn't mean she didn't copy it, knowing it would deflect suspicion."

But he sounded less certain than before. He pulled a card from his pocket and handed it to me. "In case anything else comes up. And if you're telling the truth, I'd recommend she doesn't stay here anymore alone once we release the place. Once a stalker kills, they're more likely to do it again."

13

My mom, Geoff, and Mark waited for us in Mark's hotel room when Ahanti and I arrived.

If the situation hadn't been so grim, I might have laughed at the sight they made. My mom, lipstick as fresh as if she'd applied it a moment before, sitting with her perfect posture in the desk chair. Her lilac perfume hung lightly in the air, and she hadn't even taken off her shoes to get more comfortable—that would have been unprofessional. Mark perched on the corner of the bed and shot glances at the door that connected our rooms like he was seriously considering making a break for it. Still the handsomest man I'd ever seen even when his peeling sunburn made him look like he had leprosy. And Geoff, wearing clothes that looked like he'd been heading to the gym when the police called, slouching one shoulder against the wall by the window. Between the slouch, his scowl, and his position, he reminded me a bit of a castle gargoyle.

Mark sprang to his feet and crushed me into a hug. "I hope you like gray hair, because at this rate, I'm going to be completely gray before I'm forty."

I hugged him back, even though his reaction seemed a little over the top. I hadn't been in any actual danger this time. "You'll look distinguished with gray hair anyway."

He slowly released me.

My mom pressed her lips together in a way that clearly said *what have you gotten me in to now?* "Next time, Nicole, perhaps you could be a little more detailed in your text."

What had I written? I'd been trying to contact the police, make sure we had a record of the evidence, and keep Ahanti calm all at the same time. I pulled my phone from my purse.

The text I'd sent to my mom and Mark read *Stalker broke into Ahanti's apartment with a knife. Called the police.*

I scrunched up my nose. Reading it back, I could see how that might have been misinterpreted. It did sound a bit like the stalker broke in while we were there. "Oops?"

"I assured both men that you wouldn't have taken the time to text us if the stalker had literally been in the apartment with you at that moment," my mom said.

I explained what had happened in more detail. "And I got a picture."

My mom and Mark moved forward, huddling over my phone in the slightly gruesome curiosity shared by medical examiners and criminal defense attorneys who've seen too much to be shocked by anything.

Between them I caught a glimpse of Geoff's face. He was watching us with a look that I might have given to a vampire going in for a human snack.

He moved past us to Ahanti. "We need to talk outside," he said low in his throat.

From the corner of my eye, I caught movement that I assumed was Ahanti shaking her head. "Whatever you're going to say, you might as well say in front of Nicole. I'll tell her anyway, and she'll tell Mark because couples shouldn't keep secrets."

Geoff's skin was the color of dark chocolate, making it impossible to tell if his face went red or not. "Like you kept things from me, you mean."

I might not be able to see a change in his skin color, but I could hear it in his voice. Mark and I had our own disagreements, and Geoff's voice had taken on that spoiling-for-a-fight tone people got when grievances had piled up over time. Ahanti said he hated causing a public scene, but she'd forced his hand.

Ahanti shrugged away from him. "This situation isn't easy."

"I didn't say it was, but catering to this man hasn't gotten us anywhere. We should elope the way I wanted. Once he sees you're married, he'll stop trying to win you over, and we'll be done with this."

A cold shot, like spilling ice water down my arms, ran

over me. Mark glanced up from his examination of the image on my phone's screen and met my gaze.

He caught it, too. If Geoff were Ahanti's stalker, we'd found the reason why he might have sent the burned picture of himself.

He didn't want to wait to get married. He didn't want to share their wedding with anyone else. It made me think about the stalker Taylor Swift had a few years back who believed he was married to her and who threatened to shoot anyone who he saw as a danger to her or their relationship. I wasn't up on celebrity news, but I vaguely remembered Rhianna having a similar situation.

The chill on my skin seeped into my blood, down deep to my bones. If Geoff turned out to be her stalker and she married him, she'd never be safe. Things would be okay at first, but then if he ever felt she wasn't paying enough attention to him, if he ever imagined she might be interested in another man, he could snap again and hurt Ahanti or someone else. I didn't even want to think what would happen if they had children and he felt Ahanti was paying them more attention than she paid him.

My mom passed my phone back into my numb hand. Up until this point, she'd been pretending to ignore the conversation. In my family, arguments weren't something you ever did in front of non-family. It didn't matter the impetus.

But Ahanti and Geoff weren't her family, so up until now, she'd been treating it the way she did when clients argued with their relatives in front of us. By the look on her face, her patience had run out.

She extended an arm between them like a blocker. "That's enough," she said in the tone that always made me cower as a child, even if I hadn't done anything wrong. "Whoever is behind this killed a man because that man seemed to be harassing Ahanti." She speared Geoff with the gaze that made prosecuting attorneys sit back down and forget the objection they were about to make. "Getting married could get you killed as well. In her stalker's version of reality, she wants to be with him, and you'd have coerced her into a situation the stalker would feel compelled to free her from."

Ahanti sank to the edge of the bed. Her eyes glassed over like she no longer saw anything around her.

Geoff crossed his arms over his chest. "Then we should leave DC. I can start a new practice anywhere."

My mom said something about how they'd have to change more than their location to lose a stalker determined enough to kill for her. The buzzing in my head made it hard to focus on what she was saying.

They couldn't be allowed to move away. Not until we were sure he wasn't the stalker. She'd have no one to protect her, and she wouldn't know to protect herself until it was too late.

Mark slid a hand down my arm and shook his head. He leaned in close, his lips almost touching my ear. "I know what you're thinking."

He pulled me back to the other side of the room.

"Geoff was in police custody most of today," he whispered. "He wouldn't have had time to leave the knife and photo after Ahanti left for work and before the police called him in. It wasn't him. We're still looking for someone else."

14

When Mark and I came out of the church service we'd picked to attend the next morning, Mandy had texted me. Again.

If you let me throw the nylon leashes out, I'll buy you these pretty leather leashes with the matching collars to replace them.

She sent me a link. The woman was obsessed. I only ever used the nylon leashes to tie the dogs to the stoop railing when I bathed them outside, so maybe I should let them go. The old leather leashes could be the bath leashes, and the ones Mandy had picked out were much nicer. But I'd let her stew a little longer first.

Ahanti had texted me as well.

Police done with my apartment. I called Eddie, and he's free this afternoon to check my place. Can you come?

In the second it took Mark to unlock the car with the clicker, I considered telling her no. Eddie should know more about what to check than I would. Besides, this trip was supposed to be about Mark, and so far, I hadn't even spent much time with him.

Thankfully, it didn't seem like I'd been expected to. Most of the events they'd had planned were for Mark to get a better idea of the scope of their research, the work environment, and what they were offering him. Other than the first day, and a dinner we were supposed to attend together with his potential future boss and his wife, my presence hadn't been necessary.

But still. It felt like I was spending most of my time hunting down another criminal and not nearly enough time with Mark seeing the sights. I hadn't even had time to confront my dad about blackmailing—or bribing, depending on how you looked at it—Mark into staying here.

The passenger-side window lowered. "Are you getting in?" Mark asked.

Enough heat to rival the Virginia sun arched up my neck and into my cheeks. Ahanti always teased me about my tendency to space out when I was thinking. I climbed in.

The leather seats scorched my legs even. "Ahanti's having a security check of her apartment done today. She wants me to come by."

"Should I drop you off?"

He didn't sound angry. He didn't even sound annoyed. I couldn't lean over far enough to kiss his cheek, so I snagged a hold of his nearest hand and planted a kiss on the back of that.

He flipped his hand over so ours rested palm to palm and squeezed. "We'll have to talk eventually about whether I take his job or not."

At first it felt like a topic jump. But it wasn't really. He was still thinking I wouldn't be happy long-term in Fair Haven because of how cases drew me in like they were the bright light and I was the mosquito.

"Do they want your decision before we leave?"

Mark shook his head. "They said they're slowly expanding the department, so we can take a few weeks to decide after we go home."

Mark pulled into a parking space in front of Ahanti's building. "Did you want me to stay? If not, your mom asked if I wanted to get coffee just the two of us this afternoon."

The panic sensors in my brain flashed all sorts of warning colors at the thought of Mark and my mom having coffee. For all I knew, she was in on whatever my dad's plan was. I was much more afraid of her ability to sway Mark than of my dad's.

But telling him no and making him stand around while Eddie checked Ahanti's alarm system would be selfish. "Go ahead. I'll text you when we're done."

Eddie had arrived a few minutes before me. By the time Ahanti buzzed me in and I climbed the stairs, he already had her keypad panel pulled apart.

This morning, Ahanti's face had the long appearance of someone who hadn't slept, and before I left for church, I'd noticed she wore the same clothes as yesterday. She also hadn't wanted to talk and had declined my offer of breakfast out at IHOP, even though her favorite indulgent breakfast was their cupcake pancakes.

I hadn't thought she could possibly look worse, but she did. She still wore yesterday's outfit, and she had the fidgety quality of someone who'd had twice the amount of caffeine that was healthy.

She tilted her head to the side in a *follow me* gesture, and then practically pulled me into the bathroom. She turned on the tap like we were in some sort of spy movie. "I asked Eddie to check the panel for a bug too. I couldn't stop thinking about it last night. If this guy got in here once, he could have been in here before. He might know what I'm saying because he's listening in." Her bottom lip sagged, and she glanced up at her light fixtures, then quickly away. "What if he has cameras, too?"

My own stomach corkscrewed, and I pulled her into a hug to hide any reaction.

She could be right. I should have thought of it sooner. We'd thought up a lot of ways her stalker could have knowledge of private communications. We'd talked about keystroke trackers and tapped phones. She couldn't remember where she was when she made the overheard call or wrote the compromised email, so we'd considered her stalker was in Skin Canvas and overheard the call.

Perhaps they sneaked a look at her computer while she had the email open and half written, and left it unattended.

Now that we knew they had access to her apartment, we couldn't cross off the idea that they'd had access all along.

What that meant they'd seen...the room spun slightly, and I held Ahanti tighter. "We'll figure this out. I swear it."

How was I ever going to come good on that promise? The one consolation was that her stalker clearly didn't want to share her and so they wouldn't post any still shots from a video around the internet.

For the first time in a long time, I wanted my dad. I wanted him to take over and fix this somehow.

My brain played a trick on me, conjuring my dad into the apartment. It sounded like Eddie was talking to another man out in the main room, but Ahanti hadn't buzzed anyone else in, and there was no way Eddie would have done it without asking.

Ahanti yanked away from me and lost so much color from her face you would have thought she'd donated blood three times in one day.

She'd heard the second male voice as well.

15

*E*ddie didn't sound upset, but no one else should be here. Even though I struggled to hear the voice clearly over the running water, I could tell it didn't belong to either Geoff or Mark.

I touched two fingers to Ahanti's shoulder in a *stay here* gesture.

Terrance stood next to Eddie, a set of keys still dangling from his hand.

He glanced in my direction, and his too-white-to-be-natural smile split his face. "Hey. I was just telling Eddie I didn't expect anyone to be back here. Ahanti said she was staying with you for a bit. Thought I'd stop in and water her plants."

It sounded reasonable. Sort of. Ahanti did have a collection of orchids and other high-maintenance plants along her window sills. When I was living next door, I'd been her designated waterer whenever she went out of town. She tended to leave more detailed instructions for her plants than most people left for their pets or children.

On one hand, Terrance was thoughtful to think about them and how upset Ahanti would be if one of them died before she came back.

On the other hand, it was kind of weird for him to come back to the scene of a former break-and-enter without permission. For all he knew, the police weren't even done fingerprinting the place yet. She only got the call this morning.

I caught a movement of color in my peripheral vision. Now that she'd turned off the tap, Ahanti must have recognized Terrance's voice and felt safe enough to emerge.

I was starting to wonder if that was the right call. I couldn't get past the fact that he had a key, which meant easy access to her apartment anytime he wanted.

Ahanti moved up beside me. Her gaze flickered from Eddie to Terrance to the keys in Terrance's hand. "Did you ever leave those lying around?"

Terrance flipped the keys up into his palm and closed his fingers around them. "Of course not. I'm not stupid. I got my car and apartment keys on here too."

My heart beat so fast and hard in my chest that it almost felt like it was hitting my ribs. Terrance's motives for coming here might be as innocent as he wanted them to sound, but they might not. I needed to defuse this situation. Fast.

Because if he were her real stalker, ticking him off right now was the worst possible thing we could do. Her stalker had left her what they clearly felt was a lovely present. They'd protected her. Ingratitude after that type of action could be a trigger for further violence.

I brushed my fingers against Ahanti's arm. "I'm sure he keeps his keys in his pocket like Mark does. He'd know if anyone snagged them from there." I directed my mouth into a smile. If I thought hard enough about my mom, maybe I could manage one that looked as real as hers did even when I knew they were fake. "We're going to stop in and take care of the plants, but I'll make sure she's never here alone. Thanks, though. Ahanti was just telling me how big a help it is to know that you've got the studio covered while she takes a few days off."

Ahanti and I hadn't actually talked about her taking a few days off, but I didn't want her going back to work alone with Terrance, given my newly born suspicion.

And giving him that responsibility sounded reasonable while still stroking his ego. If he were the stalker, it should be enough to keep him from doing anything else crazy until we could find some evidence to hand over to the police. Hopefully enough evidence to get a warrant for his fingerprints and kitchen knives.

His eyebrows twitched in a way that made me think he was deciding whether or not to frown.

Ahanti shifted beside me, almost leaning against me as

if her legs were fighting to keep her upright. "I don't feel well."

Her face was still pale, but I couldn't tell if she was saying that for show because I'd mentioned her taking a few days off or if she really felt unwell.

I slid an arm around her waist and moved her toward the couch.

Terrance raised a hand in the universal *see-ya* wave. "Take as long as you need. I can even call your clients and reschedule if you want."

He backed out the door.

I helped Ahanti lower to the couch. When I looked up, Eddie towered right next to us. He still held the front of the alarm panel in his hand.

My breath caught in my throat, and I coughed. Ahanti wasn't the only one getting jumpy.

"Are you alright?" he asked Ahanti.

She'd slumped her whole body back against the couch cushions. She moved her head in an almost imperceptible shake.

"Maybe you could come back and finish the check another time?" I said.

He looked between us. "Is there anything I can do to help?"

Ahanti opened her eyes. Barely. They were still more like slits. "Thank you, but no. I have Nicole."

He held up the alarm panel. "I'll put this back then."

I waited for him to finish and leave. As soon as the door

clicked shut, I went and threw the deadbolt into place. This time I added the chain as well, since Terrance had the keys. We didn't need any more surprise visitors.

Ahanti had both hands resting on her chest when I got back. "Could this be about something else?"

Her voice had a breathless quality to it, like she'd been running. I'd been hoping she'd been putting on a show for the guys, but it didn't seem like it. "What do you mean?"

"Like maybe the person who sent the obsessive messages and the person who threatened Geoff aren't the same person. Maybe that's why we can't make it all fit."

I hadn't caught anything that would suggest we were dealing with separate people, but she must have figured out something I hadn't. It wouldn't be the first time I was looking in one direction and the real culprit was hiding in another. "You'll have to explain that to me a little more."

She lowered her hands to her sides and shifted to face me. She kept her cheek leaned against the back of the couch. "Terrance...he and Geoff never...sometimes I'd loan Terrance money and he wouldn't always pay it back." Once she got going, she spit the words out fast. "Geoff didn't like it. It was the only thing we really argued about. Terrance probably guessed that I'd eventually give in to what Geoff wanted and stop loaning him cash."

Ahanti stopped talking so suddenly that I jerked forward, afraid she'd passed out, but her eyes were still open. She didn't seem to want to state the final conclusion. I'd caught up anyway.

Maybe the recent events were about breaking up her marriage rather than stalking her. I didn't want to ask how much she'd been loaning him. It had to be quite a bit or Geoff wouldn't have objected so strongly. He wasn't a stingy man. I knew he gave generously to the American Cancer Society and No Kid Hungry.

So the fact that Terrance had been borrowing a lot of money from Ahanti and that he had access to her apartment raised a whole new battery of questions. "Do you have any idea why he might have killed Cary?

She went pastier than someone with her skin tone should have been able to.

"Assuming he did," I hastily amended.

"He might have owed Cary money, too. It's not like either of them would have told me if he did."

We could sort out the motive for Cary later if we found a clear connection between Terrance and the burned photo of Geoff. What we needed now was evidence one way or the other. Otherwise, how was Ahanti ever supposed to comfortably return to working alongside him?

We could start with whether we could see a difference in what we knew the real stalker sent and what might have been done by Terrance. I pulled out my phone and brought up my photos. One thing I could say for my dad—he'd trained me well. I was happy to pass along the stalker's communications to the police because I'd already made my own records.

I pulled up the photo of the message about Geoff.

Unlike all the others, the sender had written this message in red marker rather than the generic blue ink of the earlier missives.

Ahanti leaned in. "Why change to red marker? That could mean it was written by someone else."

"It could also mean the stalker didn't have a pen handy or that he intentionally chose the marker because it seemed more threatening."

I flipped back to the other photos. The writing looked sort of the same but it was hard to tell. The writer clearly wasn't used to trying to write clearly with a fat marker. We'd need the eyes of a handwriting expert to be sure. Back home, I could have turned to Erik or some other member of the Fair Haven police department to call on an expert. Here, Detective DeGoey wasn't going to share his results with me.

But my parents had resources I didn't.

I texted my mom, asking if she could recommend someone, even though she wouldn't write back while at coffee with Mark. One of my mom's mantras was *never divide your attention because it will always halve your results.* That, and she found it rude when people paid more attention to their cell phones than the person they were with.

I zoomed in on the handwriting on the note about Cary. It was written on one of Ahanti's old pieces of scrap paper using a green pencil crayon she'd left laying out. The stalker truly must have expected to find her in her apartment and to be able to deliver his token of affection to her.

That meant he was escalating to the point where he was ready to make open contact with her. It was a dangerous moment in this kind of situation. I'd already told Ahanti that if she did come face to face with her stalker, she needed to play along with his delusion until she could get safely away. Hopefully Ahanti was able to do that.

I swiped back to one of the notes Ahanti received at the studio. They looked to be by the same hand as whoever left the knife.

"The new note about Cary looks like a match for your original stalker."

Ahanti touched my phone's screen, moving back and forth between the two. "That's a little hope at least. Isn't it? I mean, I've known Terrance for like a decade. I can see him pulling some crap, trying to break Geoff and me up, but he's no killer."

Having a copy of her key didn't mean he put the note in her apartment. *Correlation,* as my dad loved to say, *isn't the same as causation.* Just because people who smoked also tended to have high levels of alcohol consumption didn't mean that smoking caused those people to drink more alcoholic beverages.

"Has he tried anything else to break you two up?"

She stroked her fingers through her hair, like the feel of it soothed her. "Yeah. It didn't seem like a big deal before, but he liked to make nasty comments about Geoff not even letting me give him a tattoo and how it wasn't supportive. Stuff like that."

Frustration built inside me until I wanted to throw my phone across the room. If Terrance had sent the single message because he didn't want his money fountain to dry up, then he might have unintentionally escalated her real stalker. Her stalker only killed Cary because he seemed like a growing threat to Ahanti and her happiness.

The real problem was, the evidence we had could be interpreted two ways, and we couldn't know which was correct without knowing if the handwriting on the threat against Geoff matched all the rest. I'd compared hand-writing samples before and been able to tell when they matched, but the different writing tools, different colors, and closeness of the styles meant I couldn't be sure this time.

My mom still hadn't texted me back, but the coffee shop she'd suggested to Mark was about a fifteen-minute walk from here. "Why don't we meet up with my mom and Mark? I'm hoping she'll know someone we can take these handwriting samples to for some answers. Are you feeling up to a walk?"

Ahanti nodded. "Whatever it takes. I can't handle much more of this."

Just in case, we double-checked that all her windows were locked and that the door was secure behind us.

Ahanti also pushed the apartment building exterior door shut behind us. There'd always been a notice reminding residents to do so, warning them not to allow anyone they didn't know into the building. I know I hadn't been as careful about it as I should when I lived there. I couldn't have been the only one.

"I know it's Sunday," a girl's voice said behind us, "but I just wanted to talk to you for a minute and see if you'd change your mind."

Ahanti and I turned like we were synchronized swimmers. The young woman Ahanti had turned away from Skin Canvas the other day waited on the sidewalk.

Ahanti pressed both palms into the line where her forehead met her hair. "I'm not going to change my mind until you turn twenty-five, Jana. If you want a sleeve tattoo that badly that you don't want to wait, I'm sure you could find another artist with different rules."

Jana folded her hands into a praying pose. "I know I could, but I don't want another artist. I want you to do it. I've loved your art since the first time I saw some of your designs online. I even printed them off and have them on my walls."

If I'd been Ahanti, I might have given in, but I'd always been a soft touch.

"Nikki," Ahanti's voice had a struggling-to-breathe quality to it. "I need help."

My first thought was that Terrance had come back with a knife. Or that she was about to give in to Jana's request, and she didn't want to.

Then I turned to face her.

She had one hand up to her chest. "I feel funny. I need to—"

She sank to the ground.

A jolt shot through my chest, and I dropped to my knees hard, reaching for her to keep her head from hitting the pavement if she passed out. Pain careened through my knee caps.

Jana stared down at us, both hands pressed to her mouth.

"Call 911," I said. It actually might have been more like a bark, but I had bigger things to worry about than hurting her feelings.

I helped Ahanti lean back into me. Her skin was stickier than it should have been, even given the summer heat. We'd just stepped out of the air conditioning. "What's going on? Talk to me."

She took so long to answer that I wasn't even sure she was still conscious. "My hands. Numb. And chest hurts. Can't catch my breath."

She was too young and fit for a heart attack. Could someone have poisoned her?

Mentally I ran through everything she'd touched since I joined her. I'd touched all of it as well except for her tap, and someone couldn't have poisoned a tap. But we hadn't had breakfast or lunch together. If she'd eaten or drank anything, her stalker might have been able to sneak something into her food. For all we knew, her stalker was the takeout guy, and she'd gone back to the same place.

No, that couldn't be it. Her stalker wouldn't try to kill her without first attempting to make contact. In his fantasy world, he loved her and she belonged with him. Ahanti hadn't yet rejected him.

Then what was going on? And where was the stinking ambulance? If only Mark were here, he'd know the best way to stabilize her until the paramedics arrived. "Help's coming."

I looked up at Jana for confirmation. She still had the phone to her ear, talking to the dispatcher, obviously trying to describe what was happening. She nodded.

They were on the way, but as hard as I strained, I didn't hear sirens. I had to do something. "Try to take deep breaths with me."

16

Mark and Geoff had met up with me at the hospital by the time the doctor came to speak with me.

His gaze touched on the two men, and an expression that looked suspiciously like relief flashed across his face. The paranoid part of me screamed that she'd died and he was worried I'd faint when he told me. The more rational side knew it was more likely because I'd been spouting theories about poisons as soon as we reached the hospital in the ambulance. I hadn't been able to come up with any other plausible explanation for her collapse.

The doctor shook hands and reintroduced himself. He stayed standing, which seemed like a good sign. Surely if he'd had bad news that would require a long explanation, he would have taken a seat alongside us.

"She's going to be fine. All the tests on her heart came

back clear. It looks like this was a simple panic attack, so I've given her something to calm her down. You can go in to see her now if you'd like. We'll be keeping her overnight just in case."

There was nothing simple about it, I wanted to blurt out. I'd had mild to moderate anxiety attacks before, but I'd never seen or experienced anything like this.

But I didn't say any of that. Geoff already looked on the verge of a panic attack himself. Instead I thanked the doctor and followed Geoff and Mark into her room.

Ahanti wore the same drowsy expression she'd had when I brought her home from the dentist after she had her wisdom teeth out. That was back when she and Geoff were only newly dating and she hadn't wanted him to see her drooling on herself.

Geoff sank into the chair next to her bed and held her hand, but Ahanti reached out her other hand to me.

"I'm so sorry. I feel like an idiot."

I could remind her about the half-dozen much stupider things I'd done intentionally just in the past year. She'd had no control over this. "It wasn't your fault. There's no reason to feel embarrassed. Especially with all the stress you've been under."

She shook her head against the pillow. "It was seeing Jana there when she shouldn't have known where I live. I know she can't be my stalker. She's a woman, and she would have been a kid when this all started. But I started thinking that maybe she was and how I couldn't trust anyone." She shook her head again. "It was too much, and then I couldn't breathe."

It probably also wouldn't serve any purpose to tell her that her stalker could be a woman. We had no solid proof it was a man. A woman could be romantically obsessed with her as easily as a man could.

But I did agree that Jana wasn't a suspect.

Tears slid down Ahanti's cheeks. "I can't live like this."

Geoff leaned over, and she sobbed into his chest. Tears pressed against the back of my eyes, but I wouldn't join her. I couldn't.

Clearly this couldn't keep going on the way it had been. The police were investigating Cary's murder, but there was no telling how long that would take.

The very least I could do was make sure her apartment was secure—and camera-free—before she left the hospital. Eddie meant well, but he'd admitted that he hadn't been working in his field long. We needed the very best.

That meant calling my parents.

~

ACCORDING TO MARK, MY MOM PLANNED TO HEAD TO THE gym when they parted. Her phone went straight to voicemail.

"Do you know what gym your mom goes to?" Mark asked as we sat in the car in the hospital parking lot. "We could try to track her down."

I shook my head. It wasn't like my mom and I ever worked out together. I'd had a stationary bike in my apartment for the winter, and I biked outside in the summer. "She goes someplace that offers yoga classes. She says it helps her stay calm."

"That's probably about half the gyms in the city."

I could wait and hope to reach her soon enough that we could still get someone out to Ahanti's apartment today or tomorrow, but it was already getting late in the day. On a Sunday, our chances of finding someone willing to come in were already slim and got worse by the hour.

Once again, I'd have to call my dad.

As much as I'd been wishing earlier that he would come in and make this whole mess go away, I still didn't want it to look like I needed his help. I didn't want to reinforce his opinion that I wasn't capable.

But Ahanti mattered more than my pride, and last time, he had eventually agreed to assign a private investigator to her. Too bad we hadn't also given him Terrance's picture when we'd given him Cary's. This whole thing might already be over if we had. At the time, though, Terrance hadn't even been someone we considered.

My dad didn't answer his phone, either.

Unlike my mom, I did know where my dad would be on a Sunday afternoon. It was too late in the day for golf, which meant he'd either be at my parents' apartment or at their office. Since he'd taken so much time off the past couple of days, the office seemed most likely.

I put the address into our car's GPS for Mark's sake, and we easily found a parking space. My parents' office was in a business complex that housed doctor's offices and a bank, so everything else was closed today.

"Want me to come with you?" Mark asked.

Maybe it was silly—not to mention cowardly—but I did. My dad would at least have to speak to me and be civil with Mark around or risk losing face. If Edward Dawes feared anything, it was a stain on his reputation.

The escalators in the building didn't run on weekends, so we took the stairs. By the time we reached the office, I was out of breath. Only part of it was due to the hike.

My dad answered the door, wearing a polo shirt and khakis. It was about as casual as he ever got. I wouldn't have been surprised if he'd put on a suit to come down here, just in case.

"Shouldn't you be at some church service?"

To anyone else, even to Mark, it probably sounded like an innocent question. I knew better. My dad used to belittle my Uncle Stan for his faith for years before Uncle Stan's career change from cardiologist to maple syrup farmer completely dissolved their relationship. Uncle Stan used to debate with him for hours, trying to show him how logical Christianity actually was. I don't think my dad ever listened. Even though it was years ago, from what I remembered of it, Uncle Stan calmly reasoned and my dad mocked and talked over him. To him, needing to believe in a higher power was a sign of weakness.

I wasn't about to rise to his bait. "We went this morning, but then this afternoon, Ahanti ended up in the hospital."

I mentally kicked myself and prayed my dad wouldn't ask why. Succumbing to a panic attack wouldn't earn her his sympathy. Hopefully he'd assume her stalker made a move that injured her.

I wouldn't give him time to ask. I plowed forward with, "I'm going to need to keep using the investigator you assigned to this to watch a new suspect, and I need a referral to a security firm as well."

The handwriting expert I could add in later. If I tacked it on now, it'd be too big an ask, and he'd be sure to deny something, simply to make it clear that he was in control. Right now, I was only technically asking for one additional thing, and it was the one I needed most to keep Ahanti safe. Until we were sure her apartment wasn't under surveillance, she'd never be comfortable there.

My dad leaned back on his heels and crossed his arms, and the floor felt like it dropped out from underneath me. He was going to turn me down. I should have waited to talk to my mom. I could still do that and go around him, but not without further damaging our tenuous relationship.

"You can't keep expecting to use firm resources when you refuse to be a part of this practice," he said.

I wobbled slightly. It felt like I'd been shoved.

Mark's hand brushed my back as if he saw it and

wanted me to know that he had my back. Or maybe it was his way of trying to tell me not to back away from this, metaphorically or physically. Or maybe he was just afraid I might drop from all the strain of the past week.

Whatever his reason, something deep inside my chest felt like it hardened. Mark had known me for less than a year, yet he'd been by my side through every crazy thing I'd done. How much more should my dad be there for me when I asked him?

This was not how we were going to play this. My father did not get to leverage Ahanti's safety to force me into doing what he wanted. He might not agree with or like my choices, but they were my choices. If they were mistakes, they'd be my mistakes. I'd learn from them and be stronger for them.

I mimicked his pose, arms over my chest. My father only respected strength. I could give in, take his job offer, and get what I wanted for Ahanti. But he'd never respect me, and nothing about our relationship would ever get better.

No. I'd been busy and happy in Fair Haven, and even if Mark and I moved back to DC, it wasn't a given that I'd simply come crawling back to my old job. "You can't expect me to even consider returning to the firm here when you haven't given me a reason to. I don't need your job. The way I see it, you want me back much more than I want to come back." I stretched a hand in Mark's direction. "When that's the case, you woo the candidate. I'm not a penitent prodigal begging for you to take me back"—I might have taken a bit too much pleasure in the Biblical reference given his earlier jab—"so if you want me to even *consider* your job offer, you need to show me what's in it for me."

I planted my hands back on my hips. When I did that, it made me look a bit more like my mom, the one person in the world that my dad truly respected. My rant would either make him furious or finally earn a little of that same respect for me. Regardless, I wasn't going to be weak because he saw me as weak. I'd grown a lot in my time away. I knew my flaws, but I had a lot of good strengths, too. I was worth being wooed.

His stance didn't shift, but his eyes crinkled at the corners a touch. "I suppose I can start by showing you all the resources you'd have at your disposal as an attorney with our firm." He moved out of the doorway. "Come inside."

My dad arranged for the firm's security expert to be at Ahanti's apartment the next morning. It turned out I'd been right about how often they needed him. Between the death threats they received personally and the ones their clients often received as well, they practically had a firm on retainer.

I got keys from Geoff and delivered them to the security guy.

I spent the next morning with Mark, finally taking him to some of the tourist spots I'd promised. We rode up the Washington Monument and visited the Smithsonian

National Air and Space Museum and walked hand-in-hand along the Tidal Basin. If we were going to make this decision together, I wanted him to have as much knowledge of the area as possible. I hadn't hated living here. It definitely had advantages in the way of museums, art galleries, and cultural events that Fair Haven didn't.

Mark was buying us lunch at a food truck when my phone rang. Ahanti's name and picture appeared on my screen.

It was earlier than I'd expected. I'd hoped to have her apartment swept and prepped before she was ready to go home, but I hadn't received a call from the security firm yet. They had warned me that the process would take hours. When they were done, though, Ahanti would have monitored alarms on her windows as well as her door, a new lock, and she'd be able to speak and shower, secure in the knowledge that no one was watching her.

"Hey, are they discharging you now? My surprise isn't ready yet."

"Not yet." Her voice sounded tentative. "But I got a visitor."

Oh crap. What if it was Terrance? Would she be able to sound so calm if that were the case? I had told her that she needed to play along with her stalker if he ever outed himself as such. "Are you in trouble?"

"He said I'm not a suspect in Cary's death anymore, so I don't think so, but I know you've always told me police are allowed to lie. I thought it'd be better if you were here for any questions he wanted to ask me, just in case." It almost sounded like there was a smile in her voice, as if she were smiling at someone in the room with her.

Based on what she'd said, it had to be Detective DeGoey.

I waved to Mark. "No problem. We were just grabbing lunch. I'll be right there."

~

BY THE TIME WE ARRIVED, DeGOEY AND AHANTI ALMOST had the air of old friends. He vacated the chair next to her bed for me. Mark indicated that he'd wait in the hall.

DeGoey clearly hadn't been her only visitor. The bedside table had a vase of flowers, presumably from Geoff, and two cards. I peeked inside one and saw her sister Anaya's name at the bottom. Three balloons were tied to her bedrail—one covered in tiny hearts, one covered in tiny presents, and one with a giant smiley face and the words *Get Well Soon*.

Ahanti must have noticed where I'd been looking. She grinned. "Busy day. Geoff, Eddie, Anaya, and Jana have already been by. I gave Jana a little lecture about not becoming a stalker, and we compromised on me designing a beautiful small piece for her ankle. If she handles the pain and loves the tattoo, I've promised to give her the sleeve she wants once she turns twenty-one."

DeGoey cringed. "Your friend was telling me about

some of the strange things people have tattooed on their body. And where." He brought a hand up to his chest. "I got my little girl's name and birth date tattooed here, but that's as crazy as I get."

The part of my brain that my parents had trained said he could be working to build rapport so that Ahanti would let her guard down, but I didn't think that was the case this time. He'd seemed to be genuinely enjoying her company. Not surprising really. Ahanti was one of those people who could make anyone immediately feel like a valued close friend.

DeGoey pulled out a pen and notebook. "Thanks to the box of cards and letters you let us look through, we've crossed Ms. Tenali and her fiancé off our list of suspects in the murder. It seems you were right in thinking whoever is stalking her is also the man we're looking for. In the work you've been doing to locate him, have you come up with any viable leads?"

Thankfully Mark and I had eliminated Geoff. This would have been the worst possible time to drop that on Ahanti.

We didn't have much on Terrance, but it wouldn't help Ahanti's situation or the police's investigation to hold that back now. "We don't have any solid leads, though we do have a suspicion. Did you find any evidence that her home was entered by force?"

"No sign that the lock had been picked that we could

tell. All the windows were locked. The alarm company reports an entry, but the proper code was entered."

I glanced at Ahanti.

She gave the tiniest nod. "Only four people have a key to my apartment—me, Geoff, the building superintendent, and my co-worker Terrance. He takes care of my plants when I'm away."

DeGoey scribbled in his notebook. "You've said that at least some of the communication by your stalker had to have been delivered by hand. It didn't all come in the mail. Has your building's super ever come by your place of business?"

Ahanti shook her head. "Besides, he's in his sixties and devoted to his wife."

She gave DeGoey his name anyway. Seems she was done taking chances with who it might be.

DeGoey took his leave at the same time as the doctor came in. My cell phone vibrated in my purse, and I pointed my finger toward the hall to let Ahanti know I'd take the call out there so as not to be disruptive.

I didn't recognize the number. The man on the other end introduced himself as belonging to the security company my dad set me up with.

"No problem putting the additional sensors on the windows, but our sweep did turn up a device you should be aware of."

I braced my hand against the wall behind me. Ahanti's guess at how her stalker was learning about her private conversations had been reasonable, but I'd still been hoping she'd been wrong. "What kind of device?"

"Her smoke detector was swapped for one that contains a camera and microphone. Based on the location and angle, it looks like he would have been able to see her table."

That was a relief at least. He hadn't been acting as a peeping Tom and watching her in the shower. As long as she changed near her dresser, he wouldn't have been able to see that, either. It also explained how he knew things he shouldn't have been able to. Ahanti had always said that using her laptop on the couch made her back hurt, so she used her kitchen table when she wanted to work on her computer. The scary part of that was that it was yet another sign that the stalker knew her well. Somewhere along the line, she'd had to have told him that for him to know where to put his camera.

"Remote feed, I'm assuming?"

"Yeah. We'll try to trace the source, but if he's dumping it to an online storage solution, you'll need to give all this to the police and hope they can get a warrant for the account holder. Want me to try to trace it anyway or leave that for the cops?"

A private contractor would likely get answers faster than an overworked police force. "Get me the source, then I'll hand it over to the police."

Since the camera alone didn't give us anything new on the identity of her stalker, I decided to wait until they'd traced it back before updating DeGoey. On the drive to Ahanti's apartment, though, I filled her in on what we'd done to make her home safer.

One thing that'd been bothering me since the break-in was how the perpetrator got in without her alarm system going off. One theory was the windows since they weren't linked to the alarm. The other was that the stalker already had the code. The alarm company had now confirmed that the system triggered, but someone turned it off.

"The security firm recommend changing your alarm code every week," I said. "Has it been changed since you installed it?"

She shook her head. "Terrance has the code," she said softly. "But my super doesn't. If I know he's coming, I leave the alarm off. I should have told the detective that, but I forgot."

"I'll call him later and let him know."

She accepted that without question. I also needed to still tell her about the worst of it. I waited until Mark went to get us dinner. She went through a similar range of emotions to what I had in being relieved the guy hadn't been taping a more private area of her home but also upset that someone had managed to set up a recording device in the first place.

We'd cracked open our take-out containers when my cell rang. I didn't even want to think about the long-distance charges for this visit. I hadn't expected to use my phone much at all away from home.

My caller ID told me it was the police station.

Ahanti glanced over. "You might as well put it on speaker."

Now that she knew the worst, I didn't see a reason not to. I let DeGoey know who was on my end as soon as I answered, and I filled him in on what my security pro had found.

"I'll have someone connect with him," DeGoey said. "We're going to want to take it from here. We've made an arrest."

17

*A*hanti dropped the Kung Pao chicken container she'd been holding. It hit the table with a *whap*, still upright. "Who?"

"Terrance Moore."

Ahanti put her head down on the table.

I rested a hand on her shoulder. For her sake, and for Terrance's, we had to be sure the police weren't making a mistake. "Are you able to share with us what you found that led to the arrest?"

"His fingerprints were on the photo where someone had burned out her fiancé's face. When we questioned him about it, he finally admitted to sending it."

A little moan came from Ahanti. She must feel a lot like I would if I found out that she'd been doing something like this to me.

Except we'd suspected Terrance might have sent that

single messages but not any of the others. "Were his finger-prints on any of the other messages?"

"We're still processing them. Many of them are so old that we're not expecting anything other than smudged partials."

Even if some of those belonged to Terrance, it didn't mean he'd written them. Ahanti could have shown them to him before taking them home. My prints would be on many of them from when we'd sorted them out.

We needed something more solid before we could be confident that Ahanti was safe and this was over. DeGoey didn't have the same personal stakes.

"What about ties to Cary's murder?"

"When we started investigating the murder, one of the victim's clients said they'd heard him arguing with a black man about money. They picked Terrance Moore out of a lineup this afternoon."

That made it a lot more likely that Terrance had been behind this all along.

"I'm confident he's our guy," DeGoey said. "More now than ever thanks to you finding that camera. Our background check into him showed he did one year of Computer Science at Northern Virginia Community College, and his apartment was full of gadgets. Probably what he was spending all the money he was borrowing from the victim on. He even had a high-tech drone that my guys say has to be worth nearly five grand. Once I get ahold of that camera your people found, I can see if any of the places he was buying this stuff from show a purchase for the same make and model."

I thanked him and disconnected.

Ahanti propped up her chin on her arms, her face no longer buried. "At least it's over. I can sleep tonight in my own home and walk to work tomorrow without worrying someone's going to grab me on the way. There's just one more thing I still need to do."

She grabbed her bag from the back of the chair and fished out her phone.

I was sitting close enough that I could easily read what she was typing. At first, I kept my eyes averted, thinking she was sending a message to Geoff. Then I saw the name at the top of the screen—Terrance.

Come by the studio in the next 48 hours to get your stuff or I'm throwing it out. And I want my keys back.

She added a swear word onto the end.

I reached out a hand to stop her from sending it, but I was too late.

Setting aside the practical element that Terrance might not be able to make bail—at least not in 48 hours—there was still the fact that she shouldn't have anything to do with him. I understood the rush of boldness that came with knowing your opponent and feeling you had the upper hand. Over the past few months, I'd also learned that the farther away from murderers you could stay, the better.

"I still have the private investigator sitting on Terrance. Why don't we pack up his stuff into a box and have the PI give it back to him? I'll tell him to get the keys for your apartment and Skin Canvas from Terrance at the same time."

The old defiance was back in Ahanti's face. "Now that they know who he is, he can't hurt me anymore."

That was so far from true that I didn't know where to start, but I also didn't want to send her into another panic attack. A stalker who received a text like she sent could easily become even more dangerous. She'd rejected him. He could also feel like he had nothing to lose. He was potentially going to prison for one murder. Why not two?

I couldn't say any of that. I'd have to come at it a different way—one she couldn't argue with. "It's not about that. You don't want to hurt the case against him by having any contact with him. His attorney could argue that you clearly don't believe the charges against him or you wouldn't have allowed him anywhere near you afterward."

"I can see your point, but I already texted him."

"Give me his number. I'll text him about the change in plans."

~

I WENT TO WORK WITH AHANTI THE NEXT DAY TO HELP HER package up everything that belonged to Terrance. She'd started rebooking her cancelled appointments, beginning with a design session with Jana. In the gaps between sessions, we emptied out Terrance's drawers.

Ahanti's way of dealing with it was to dump everything none-too-gently into the box.

By four in the afternoon, all Terrance's stuff was in three large boxes, sealed with packing tape. I snagged the permanent marker away from Ahanti before she wrote anything nasty on the boxes.

Eddie showed up shortly before five. He came in the door sideways, looking back over his shoulder. "There's some guy sitting out front of here in his car, watching the door. You want me to get rid of him?"

I already knew it was the private investigator. I'd asked him to drop the surveillance on Terrance, since he wouldn't see much while he was in custody anyway, and hang out here for the day, in case Terrance made bail and decided to show up.

Eddie could have at least waited until he was inside the tinted windows to point the guy out, though. If he had been someone unsavory, he'd have tipped him off. Maybe that was the idea. Let him know he was being watched to scare him away.

I stacked the final box of Terrance's stuff by the door. "We know. He's extra protection in case Terrance shows up."

Mark had insisted on it. He said if my dad balked, he'd pay for it himself. I wouldn't be much protection to Ahanti if Terrance showed up with a gun or a knife.

Eddie's frown added wrinkle rolls to his forehead, like he had too much skin there. "Terrance?"

Ahanti motioned for him to sit. "The police arrested Terrance. Nicole's fiancé was worried he might come back here and do something to hurt us. Nicole had the security people her dad's firm uses come in, and they even found a camera in my apartment. So much for him being my friend."

Eddie's mouth opened in a way that reminded me of a bear about to growl, lips pulled back and showing too many teeth. "I thought he was my friend, too."

My phone rang in my pocket. The caller ID listed a 703 area code, which meant it was DC-based. Probably the security firm letting me know they'd turned everything over to the police. I didn't want to answer it in front of Eddie and upset him more. The man looked like he might burst a vessel in his head.

I motioned to them that I was going to take it outside.

"Is this Nicole?" a man's voice said when I answered.

A man's voice that sounded too close to Terrance's for comfort.

"I need to find a lawyer," he said. "I need you to recommend a lawyer who's good and affordable. I know I can't afford your dad or anyone like that."

It was Terrance. Maybe he thought that because I'd moved to a small town I'd be easy to deceive now. That said, I also didn't want to antagonize a stalker who'd already killed someone. He'd eventually be out on bail, and even though I was headed home in a couple of days, Ahanti would still be here.

I made a you've-got-to-be-kidding-me face before I spotted Lucas, the private investigator, watching me.

I mouthed the words *Peeping Tom*.

He smirked and looked away.

"Nicole, are you still there?" Terrance asked.

I sighed. What was it about me that made all these people call me? Maybe my parents' genes emitted some sort of criminal-enticing pheromones and that was part of their success secrets. Unfortunately for Terrance, he'd called the wrong Fitzhenry-Dawes. "I'm still here, but I'm not sure why you're calling me for help. The police can set you up with a great public defender if you're not able to afford a lawyer."

"I'm a black man covered in tattoos. Jurors are going to assume I did it without even listening. I need someone great."

He didn't sound delusional. He sounded like he'd thought this through. Maybe I didn't need to cater to him quite as much. "Ahanti is my best friend."

"She's my friend too. You don't think I really did this, do you?"

"They have your fingerprints on the picture of Geoff with the threat written on the back."

In the silence that followed, I caught voices in the background. Wherever he was, he wasn't back at his apartment. He might still be at the police station, and I was the call he made to try to find a lawyer to help him when he went before a judge. If he'd been smart, he would have asked for a lawyer when the police first started to question him.

Not if he was innocent, the annoying voice in my mind that loved to play devil's advocate said. *Innocent people often don't think to ask for a lawyer until it's too late.*

It had been the first time in memory that Terrance had asked a question and waited for me to finish it. This time he cared about my answer. That was out of character enough to make me less confident than I had been before my phone rang that he was our guy.

Terrance cleared his throat in an awkward, phlegmy way. "I sent that one message. I'll admit that. I was overdrawn on all my cards. I didn't want to break them up permanently. Just a little longer until I could get back on my feet. I didn't kill Cary, and I'm not some crazy stalker. Ahanti isn't even my type."

I'd only met one of Terrance's girlfriends over the years, and she'd had a lot more in the way of curves than Ahanti. But one voluptuous girlfriend didn't prove he wasn't obsessed with Ahanti. "Are you saying you didn't owe Cary money?"

The silence stretched out again. "I owed him money, yeah."

He wasn't giving me much to go on. "Can you give me a clear reason that I should believe the police are wrong?"

This time he didn't say anything at all. A lot of my parents' clients—ones I knew were guilty—told even their friends and family that they were innocent. My dad would happily tell you how few were. I think he actually preferred it that way. The challenge was higher, but the stakes were lower. In a way, for him, defending someone who was guilty was a win either way. If he lost, a criminal went to prison. If he won, his reputation went up. And he got paid either way.

I was not my father. If Terrance couldn't convince me he was innocent, I wasn't going to help him. "I'm sorry, Terrance. I have to go."

I disconnected before he could say anything else.

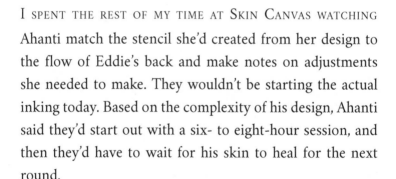

I SPENT THE REST OF MY TIME AT SKIN CANVAS WATCHING Ahanti match the stencil she'd created from her design to the flow of Eddie's back and make notes on adjustments she needed to make. They wouldn't be starting the actual inking today. Based on the complexity of his design, Ahanti said they'd start out with a six- to eight-hour session, and then they'd have to wait for his skin to heal for the next round.

I left Ahanti safe under the watchful eyes of Eddie and the private investigator to get ready for dinner out with Mark's potential future boss and his wife.

With all that had gone on in the past few days, I'd completely forgotten to ask Mark about his coffee date with my mom. He hadn't come out of it with the same I-need-to-think expression as he had his golf round with my dad, so I'd already guessed she hadn't said anything too shocking. Still, my curiosity couldn't let it go at that.

Once we were on our way and sitting in traffic, it seemed as good a chance as any to ask. Especially since Mark looked like he was verging on turning into the Hulk, road-rage version, again.

"Did you and Mom have a good time on Sunday?" I realized belatedly how stupid that sounded considering they'd ended up cutting it short so Mark could join me at the hospital. "I mean, did she behave herself?"

Arg. That didn't sound much better. That made it sound like I expected her to flirt with him or something. The subtle approach was clearly not going to work for me today.

Mark glanced sidelong at me, his scowl replaced with a dimpled grin. At least my garbled speech worked as a distraction. "In other words, did your mom try to bribe or bully me the way your dad did?"

I faked an I-don't-know shrug.

Mark chuckled. "Her approach was different, but I think they're united in wanting us to move here. She asked how I liked the position I'd been offered, and then she wanted to know what I thought your biggest objections to moving back to the DC area were."

That was a different tactic, but it didn't surprise me as much as it might have. My mom was incredibly adaptable. She'd set out to deconstruct me the same way she did opposing arguments since I opposed her desire.

"And what did you tell her?"

"That I could see myself enjoying the work and the people I'd be working with."

I stuck my tongue out at him. Not only was that not what I meant, but I knew that already. Mark and I had talked a lot about how he felt about the job offer while we were enjoying the sights on Monday. "What did you tell her about me?"

"I said you'd miss the friends you'd made in Fair Haven."

He was spot-on with that one, but moving back to DC meant being closer to my mom and Ahanti, and even my dad, all of whom I also missed. Too bad my mom couldn't find jobs in Virginia for everyone I loved. "What else?"

"I said you were worried about Velma and Toby having enough space in the city. You didn't want them to be stuffed into an apartment."

Even though the apartment I'd lived in before had been spacious by DC standards, I couldn't imagine Mark, me, a Great Dane, and a Bullmastiff all crammed into it. Plus, Toby was an older dog with a back leg that sometimes gave him trouble. If we got a place where he had to navigate more than a few stairs, that could become a major problem the older he got.

"I also said you'd never be happy in a career where you had to defend people who are guilty. It's not who you are."

That one would have been the hardest for my mom to take. It had been when I'd told her something similar when she'd come to visit. She was convinced I'd one day be able to overcome my struggles speaking in front of a jury. She couldn't change my personality, though, and I had to end my days proud of the work I'd done. I couldn't say I'd made the world a better place if my job was freeing criminals.

"Is that it?"

He nodded. "Unlike me, you seem to have as many things you like about city living as you do about small-town life."

He hadn't mentioned Sugarwood at all. Surely I'd miss Sugarwood. I closed my eyes and imagined the things I loved about it, but all that came into my mind were my horses, the people, and the trees. I wasn't attached to the work there at all, and with Stacey wanting to take on more and more responsibilities alongside Russ, pretty soon they wouldn't even need me. Stacey, much to the chagrin of my ego, was better at my roles there than I was. Not only that, but she loved them more.

Despite the fact that we were meeting for dinner in Annapolis, Maryland, an hour from DC, I still hadn't worked it all through in my head by the time we arrived. Mark parked the car, and we strolled along the red brick streets and down by the water. Despite its size, this part of Annapolis had always felt full of Old World charm to me. I'd rarely had the time to make the drive back when I lived and worked in the DC area, unfortunately.

The little Italian restaurant Mark's potential future boss had picked out served delicious penne, and they were a couple I could see us becoming friends with if we moved back to DC.

That in itself was a strange thought. The people here would only ever have known us as Nicole and Mark together. Back in Fair Haven, our friends had known us separately as well.

My phone vibrated in my purse as we were finishing dessert. Since Mark's boss' wife had left for the restroom, I excused myself from the table. The private investigator was supposed to call me when he'd delivered Terrance's belongings to him, and I wanted to make sure it was done. Once it was, Terrance wouldn't have any legitimate reason for returning to Skin Canvas, and Ahanti could immediately call the police if she saw him hanging around.

The number on my screen did belong to the PI I'd hired. Answering with *Is it done?* sounded a little too mafia-ish, so I opted for the old standby. "Fitzhenry-Dawes."

"It's Lucas, ma'am. I didn't know if you'd get a call from the police or not, so I thought I should check in with you."

It was a good thing I hadn't stayed at the table. I was pretty sure I currently wore an *oh crap* expression. It couldn't be Ahanti. If anything had happened to her, Geoff would have called me, not the PI. "What's going on?"

"After your friend went home, I took the boxes to the guy's address like you told me. He didn't answer when I knocked, so I waited around for him to come back. Turns out I wasn't the only one. Before I could get out of my car, some guy jumped him."

For a second, I felt like I'd walked into a glass door—dazed and confused. Thankfully, he seemed to interpret my silence as a sign to continue.

"I scared the attacker off, but the guy you had me sitting on was sliced up pretty bad. He lost a lot of blood before paramedics got to us."

Sliced up...that sounded like... "The guy who jumped him tried to kill him with a knife?"

"That's what it looked like to me. They took me in the ambulance since I got cut across the hand, but nobody here'll tell me anything about the other guy. All I can tell you was he was still breathing when we got to the hospital."

"Did you get a good look at the attacker? Could you identify him?"

"Sorry, ma'am. It happened too fast."

I sank into the empty chair nearest to me. Someone had tried to kill Terrance. Likely the same person who'd killed Cary. If Ahanti's stalker and Cary's murderer were the same person, then Ahanti's stalker had tried to kill Terrance.

Terrance wasn't Ahanti's stalker after all.

18

One of the least flattering qualities I'd inherited from my dad was how difficult it was for me to apologize. Perhaps it was because it meant admitting I'd fallen short. I'd worked hard to apologize when I was wrong, but it still never felt comfortable.

Even less so when my mistake landed someone in the hospital. Mark tried to convince me on our drive back to DC that Ahanti's stalker would have attacked Terrance whether or not I believed him. Maybe that was true, but maybe not. Maybe he would have been watching his back, expecting the stalker to come after him the way he came after Cary.

Maybe he would have even been somewhere else, preparing a defense.

Or maybe he'd be dead because you wouldn't have sent the

private investigator after him, the rational voice in my head said.

Even if I couldn't have known for sure what was coming, I'd let him down by not considering that he might be telling me the truth.

Which was why we were now standing in the hospital instead of heading back to our hotel. Lucas had been able to tell me where the ambulance took them, but he hadn't known anything more about Terrance's room number…or even whether he'd pulled through. The hospital could give him blood, but if the knife hit an organ, they might not have been able to save him. And I didn't know what long-term damage extreme blood loss might cause. For all we knew, Terrance could have brain damage if he survived.

Mark came back to where I'd been waiting. When I was turned away peremptorily, he'd gone back to talk to the woman at the desk. We'd wagered that either his dimples or his MD might get us a little more information.

"As a professional courtesy, they told me Terrance is alive but in critical condition. They're not allowing him visitors at this time. That's all they were willing to say."

It wasn't much, but at least he had a chance. As my dad liked to say, it's not over until the verdict is read, and even then, there are appeals.

"Should we tell Ahanti?" Mark asked.

My gut reaction was to say no since it'd destroy the modicum of peace she'd found in knowing who was stalking her. If I didn't, though, she wouldn't be paying attention anymore, and that was even more dangerous than the possibility of another panic attack.

I dialed her number. "Is Geoff with you?" The last thing I wanted to do was give her the news over the phone if she were alone.

"Yeah, we were celebrating." Her voice sounded so unsuspicious that pain bloomed in my chest. "Did you want to talk to him?"

Coward that I was, I almost considered it. I could tell Geoff and he could tell Ahanti. But if I couldn't be there for my best friend, I didn't deserve to have one. "No, I just wanted to make sure you weren't there by yourself."

A beat of silence. "That sounds a lot like a version of *are you sitting down? What's wrong?*" All the lightness drained out of her voice.

I explained what had happened to Terrance.

She didn't respond right away, but I could hear sniffling on the other end and then Geoff asking what happened. I listened as Ahanti repeated what I'd said. Geoff swore.

It was his voice when someone finally came back to the phone. "The guy you hired is sure it was Terrance who got jumped? And the police don't think it was a random mugging or something like that?"

I hadn't talked to the police. "I'll check with Detective DeGoey, but the investigator I hired knew what Terrance looked like and he helped him until paramedics arrived. It was definitely Terrance."

"I don't think Ahanti should go into work tomorrow.

Or at all, until the police figure out who's doing this. It's not safe."

"I can't live like a bird in a cage," Ahanti said in the background. "I can't afford to keep cancelling appointments. I've worked too hard to flush away my business. Nikki even said I'm not the one who's done anything wrong."

The hysterical note in her voice sounded like it might be helped along by a couple glasses of alcohol. Geoff had probably brought champaign, thinking this was all behind them at last.

"Do you hear that?" Geoff asked me. "Reason with her. Maybe she'll listen to you."

Muffled noises like they were passing the phone back and forth, Geoff insisting she talk to me again, and Ahanti refusing to accept it from him. They'd definitely both had a couple of glasses of something. Neither of them were heavy drinkers, and they both tended to get a little goofy when they did drink.

"I'm going into work tomorrow," Ahanti finally said into the phone. "I think the reason I had that panic attack was because I was focusing so hard on guarding my every move. It's too stressful for me to live a half-life like that."

Couples had broken up over smaller trials than this. I didn't want that for them. They really were good for each other. And one of their strengths as a couple was compromising. I just had to get them to remember that.

Surely the attack on Terrance had given the police

more evidence they could use to figure out who was really behind this. They'd have to believe Terrance's story that he sent only the one message, trying to break up Ahanti and Geoff. What we needed to do was find a way to keep Ahanti safe until the police analyzed the new evidence, but we had to do it in a way that made her not feel so trapped.

"Put me on speaker, okay?"

"I think that worked," Ahanti said, her voice sounding farther away.

I put my end on speaker as well so Mark could hear. "How many clients do you have booked for tomorrow?"

"Two. A design consult for a new client and then Eddie's back in. I'm starting his tattoo tomorrow."

That wasn't nearly as bad as it could have been. For tomorrow at least, it'd be easy enough to keep Ahanti safe at work, especially if I could get Lucas to sit out front again. "You want to work, and Geoff wants to keep you safe. After your consult leaves and Eddie arrives, could you lock the door and turn your sign to closed? That way no one unexpected can walk in on you."

"Without Terrance there, that'd be best anyway. I can't stop what I'm doing whenever someone comes in."

"What about with the new client?" Geoff said. "That could be her stalker."

With how her stalker had escalated and the content of his messages, I doubted it. They'd talked about Ahanti's touch. A new client wouldn't have even sat down to talk with her yet.

Geoff wouldn't see it that way, though.

I glanced at Mark. I hadn't spent much time with him this trip, not the way we'd planned, at least.

He moved in behind me and wrapped his arms around my waist. "We'll make sure she's not there alone with the new client."

By the time we finished the call to Ahanti and Geoff, it was almost midnight. I went back to my room, but instead of crawling into bed like any sane person would do, I pulled Detective DeGoey's card from my wallet.

I turned it end over end. He shouldn't have given it to me if he didn't intend for me to call. But it was late, and the intent behind it had been for me to call if I had any more information about the case, not for me to call because I *wanted* information about the case.

Manners won out, and I set the card on my nightstand. Ahanti was safe in her apartment with Geoff, and nothing the detective said could make a difference tonight anyway.

19

I slept fitfully, waking up from nightmares I couldn't remember. I ended up out of bed and showered before my alarm was even set to go off. That gave me the vague sensation that I was doing vacationing wrong. Then again, there'd been nothing else normal about this trip.

Mark and I planned to stay with Ahanti until her consult client left and Eddie arrived, and then we'd made an appointment with a realtor to find out about house prices within an easy commute of where Mark might end up working. He'd been right when he said one of my major concerns was apartment living with two big dogs. If we couldn't afford a house with even a modest yard within a close enough distance that Mark wouldn't give himself high blood pressure thanks to the traffic, that would be a major black mark against moving back to DC. Most people likely would have waited until they'd decided to move before pricing homes, but I wasn't most people. I liked having a plan, and I hated surprises.

Ahanti opened late on Wednesdays, so I waited until Mark and I had breakfast together before calling Detective DeGoey. By the time I woke up this morning, I'd realized that the grumpier he was, the less likely I was to get any information from him. Waking him up accidentally seemed like a great way to increase the grumpy factor.

DeGoey answered on the second ring.

"This is Nicole Fitzhenry-Dawes, Ahanti Tenali's lawyer."

"I remember you." His voice had a dry edge to it, but I couldn't tell if amusement or annoyance put it there. Police officers had enough training in controlling their tells that they were harder to read even in person, let alone on the phone.

Which left me with no direction as to how to forge ahead. "We learned about Terrance Moore and—"

"I can't talk to you about an ongoing investigation."

That was vague enough to make me want to shake him. Was he referring to the investigation into who had attacked Terrance? Or was he trying to tell me without telling me that they were reopening the investigation into Cary's murder?

I'd assume it was a hint if I was back in Fair Haven where even I-never-jaywalk Erik fudged things a little to give me information. But we weren't in Fair Haven anymore, Toto.

Unfortunately, that also meant I couldn't be Fair Haven Nicole. Here I had to be Big City Nicole. I hadn't had much success at that before. If you asked my parents, succeeding here required a drive and hardness that I didn't have. And didn't want to have.

But now was as good a time as any to see if I could get what I wanted and needed here without sacrificing who I was.

"I appreciate that, Detective. I don't want to impede your investigation in any way or jeopardize a conviction when you find the right suspect. All I've ever wanted was to make sure whoever is behind this is caught so my client can be safe."

I made sure to keep any snark or snootiness out of my voice. I didn't want to imply that he didn't care about justice or about Ahanti's safety. It seemed to me like he did care.

The silence on his end of the line stretched like I'd caught him off guard. He'd probably expected some moral blackmail like *I hope you can appreciate that we can't trust you to keep people safe and to find the right perpetrator.* In the background, I heard the low drone of a room full of people talking, but none of them close enough to hear distinct words.

I forged ahead. "I'm calling because we'd like to know if the attack on Terrance yielded any more evidence that might point you to who's really behind this. We need to know how extreme we need to get in making sure my client stays safe. I figured that if I tried to work with you instead of against you, there'd be a better chance of achieving that."

The noise in the background faded as if DeGoey were moving away from a group of people. "Take whatever precautions you can. I'm doing what I'm able to on my end, but my opinion of what's going on isn't the popular one anymore. Recent events might end up being treated as an unrelated crime."

He'd kept it vague enough that he couldn't be accused of giving me anything he shouldn't. I understood anyway. He believed Terrance wasn't the guy, but it was possible he'd be outvoted and Terrance, if he survived, might still be tried for Cary's murder and for stalking Ahanti. That likely meant the attack on Terrance hadn't turned up any new evidence, at least not yet. It could take weeks before they had the DNA results from the lab.

Worse, unless something changed, we were on our own for figuring out who was really behind it all.

∼

"I DON'T KNOW WHAT TO DO NEXT," I SAID TO MARK AS WE drove to Skin Canvas. "Since Terrance sent the picture of Geoff, the list Ahanti made earlier isn't even a starting point. Her stalker might have been there that day, but he might not."

The only thing we knew for sure anymore was that her stalker was a man. My private investigator was sure the attacker was a man.

With only a couple of days left before Mark and I headed back to Fair Haven, it didn't look like we were going to solve this before we had to leave. Detective DeGoey hadn't sounded confident that the police would pursue other suspects. And Ahanti would remain at risk, the focus of a man who'd killed already.

"When we eliminate what Terrance sent, what do we still know?" Mark asked.

The words *not much* came to mind, but that wasn't entirely true. "Many of the messages still showed up at Skin Canvas, and the stalker wrote to her about her touch, so it's likely one of her clients."

Mark gave an affirmative grunt and hit the brakes to avoid a car that jammed itself into a space that barely fit it. "What I do sometimes is look at anything strange that doesn't seem to fit, and I focus on that."

The fact that he could still come up with that while navigating the traffic was impressive.

The thing that had troubled me since we first catalogued this creep's messages were the strange gaps. "He doesn't maintain consistent communication with her."

"It could be someone who travels for work," Mark said.

I pulled my phone from my purse and opened the note feature. I typed in Mark's suggestion. "It probably isn't multiple incarcerations. She'd know if one of her clients kept ending up in jail." I tapped the edge of my phone against my chin. There wasn't much in the way of specifics in the messages, but the comments about her touch still made my skin crawl. "Maybe he sends her messages either when she's working on one of his tattoos or when she isn't."

"Isn't would make more sense." Mark parked the rental car. "If she's as much a pack rat about her calendars as she was about her fan mail, you should be able to see if any names come up regularly shortly before she received a message. Did you want me to stay and help you sort through?"

It would make the work go faster since Ahanti wouldn't be able to help. Unfortunately, it would also mean he wouldn't be able to scope out the real estate situation for us. That would make the decision about whether or not to move even harder than it would already be. And if he stayed, Ahanti would ask questions. "I don't want to get her hopes up if this turns out to lead nowhere. She must already feel like a yoyo with all the ups and downs."

Finding a parking space almost made us late. I waved at Lucas sitting in his car out front as we passed. He raised his bandaged hand in return. I couldn't keep a private investigator sitting out front of Ahanti's shop forever—at least not on my dad's dime—but, thankfully, Lucas agreed to come back today, despite the short notice.

Inside, Mark and I sat in the cushy chairs Ahanti kept in her waiting area and looked through her portfolio as if we were a couple intending to design matching tattoos. Ahanti did her consult with the new client.

The new client at least didn't strike me as a viable suspect. He wanted Ahanti to ink a picture of his wife and two kids on his back.

Mark left to meet the realtor as soon as the new client was safely out the doors. Ahanti locked the door behind him and went back to her chair to finish her notes and see when she could fit another client into her schedule.

I peeked sidelong at the calendar. Because she liked to keep everything, Ahanti still used a paper and pen planner to schedule all of her appointments. I'd be out of luck if she kept them at her apartment.

I meandered back into the office area as if I were simply killing time until Eddie arrived.

Ahanti labeled everything, so she should have it clearly marked if the calendars were here. I knelt down by the filing cabinet and opened the bottom drawer.

"What are you doing?" Ahanti said from behind me.

I lost my balance and grabbed for the filing cabinet drawer. It pulled all the way out, metal screeching against metal. I stayed upright. Barely.

Ahanti stood over me. Her arms were crossed, but another expression flickered across her face. Like for a second she was afraid she couldn't trust even me.

The part of me that always felt not quite good enough

ached in protest. The more rational part of me knew I might feel exactly the same way if our roles were reversed. Maybe more so since I was naturally paranoid and suspicious.

I clambered to my feet and brushed off my knees. Mark should have stayed because I was going to have to tell Ahanti, after all. "I was looking for your old calendars. I thought that I could use them to figure out whose appointments matched the pattern of the stalker's messages."

Her bottom lip jutted the tiniest bit. "Why were you doing it behind my back?"

This was quickly turning into one of those situations where in trying not to harm, I'd ended up doing more harm than if I'd been honest in the first place. Note to self —don't try to keep secrets from your best friend or you might not have one once it's over. "I didn't want to get your hopes up. It might be another dead end."

Ahanti cringed slightly. *Dead* end might not have been my best choice of words.

A knock sounded on the front door.

"That'll be Eddie." Ahanti pointed at the second drawer up. "The calendars are in there."

She turned on her heel. Based on the lingering sharpness to her tone, I'd need to apologize again later, once Eddie was gone.

I opened the second drawer. Laying in a neat row inside were nine planners.

I wriggled them out and took them to Ahanti's desk. I opened my phone to the notes I'd taken.

The first message from the stalker had come right after Ahanti had left Cary's studio, but that wouldn't point to anyone since it was linked to a move she'd made in her life.

I checked the month that the second note came, opened the planner for that year to the month before, and wrote down all the names. I did the same for the following month. He might have sent the message a few weeks after his appointment or a few days. By cataloguing the names in both months, I'd spread the net wide enough to capture his name either way.

The list was long, despite the fact that she was technically a new business. Many of her clients would have followed her from Cary's, though.

Terrance's name was on the list. I touched the tip of my pen to the paper beside it. My hand itched with the desire to cross it out. It'd be much easier to convince the police that Terrance wasn't their only possible suspect if he didn't correlate with the missives at all.

But if I omitted it and they found out, everything else I'd done would be called into question. Besides, this was only the first month. Eddie's name was on the list, too, along with a couple of other regulars I remembered from when I used to hang around the studio. Obviously, they weren't all guilty.

This wasn't about one month. It was about the larger pattern.

After the fifth note, the list had dwindled to half. I crossed off any names that didn't appear in a month when a note was delivered. Sadly, that still amounted to a lot of names. Including Terrance's.

What I'd failed to take into account was that many people would be on the same schedule if they liked the complex tattoos Ahanti was known for. They needed design work ahead of time. Plus, many had to be done in stages, allowing the skin to heal in between. It seemed like a lot of Ahanti's projects stretched out over months.

I rubbed at my eyes. When I dropped my hands, Ahanti stood in the doorway. "Eddie and I were wondering how it's going."

Her voice was the kind of soft people got when she wanted to put a tiff behind them without actually talking about it. Even though we hadn't had a real argument, I was just as happy to move forward.

Might as well put the best possible spin on it. "I've already eliminated half the names on my initial list. I should have it down to one or two solid possibilities to give to the police by the end of the day."

Her smile said *thank you for everything* even though she never actually said the words.

She ducked back out of the room, but returned a minute later. "I'm going to run across the street and grab us some subs for a late lunch. You want me to get you one? I think we could all use some food before we get back to it."

My mouth watered before I could form a conscious

response. A glance at my watch told me I'd already been at it two hours. No wonder Ahanti had cooled off.

I pushed back the chair and joined her in the main room. Eddie'd been face down on the table. He maneuvered to a sitting position with the cautiousness of someone with a bad sunburn. His back probably didn't feel much better than if that was what he had. The brief glance at his skin showed a huge red patch where Ahanti'd been working.

I shuddered and averted my eyes.

Ahanti handed Eddie a slip of paper to write his order, and he passed it along to me.

My eyes struggled to focus. Something niggled at my mind, and the tightness in my throat that often preceded an anxiety attacked clawed at me.

I drew a stabilizing breath and scribbled down my order. It was probably just the fear that I might soon need glasses. It wasn't ego that made me hate the thought. It was that it'd get expensive fast if I misplaced my glasses as often as everything else.

The tightness moved down my throat, into my chest, as I finished writing down what I wanted. Maybe it wasn't the prospect of glasses. Maybe what was bothering me was that Ahanti sounded like she planned to go for the subs herself rather than letting me or Eddie or Lucas go.

I kept hold on the paper. "Wouldn't it be better if I picked up the order?" I held out the paper and pen to her. "You could write down what you want."

Ahanti grabbed the paper, leaving the pen behind. "I told you last night. I'm not going to be a prisoner in my life. It was turning me into a wreck. You can watch me go and come back from the front window. It's perfectly safe."

I couldn't stop her if she'd made up her mind. Blocking the door physically would only make her angry, and she could still go out the back door.

Perhaps if it was two against one. I gave Eddie a help-me-out-here eyebrow raise.

Ahanti was already halfway to the door. "Don't think he'll back you up. He thinks it's a good idea to live my life as normally as possible."

What the heck, Eddie! He should know better considering Ahanti had told him about Cary. Since she'd told him what I was working on, presumably he knew about Terrance as well.

"Take Lucas," I yelled after her just before the front door swished shut.

Whether she signaled Lucas or he heard me, he climbed out of his car and trailed after her. I watched them cross the street, then spun back around with a scowl.

Eddie stood right behind me, looking out the front door as well. A little too close behind me.

"She's safe," he said. "I won't let anyone hurt her."

My skin felt like it was trying to shiver off my arms. That assertion sounded a lot more like it was directed at me than at Ahanti's stalker.

I stepped back, but there was only so far I could go. The

door stopped my progress, and I couldn't open it without either moving forward or to the side. Why hadn't I gone with Ahanti?

Eddie didn't come any closer.

Maybe I was overreacting. This situation hadn't been as stressful on me as on Ahanti, but according to my counselor, I had a mild case of PTSD from everything I'd been through. It wasn't impossible that I was reading too much into Eddie's voice and body language.

I shifted to face him, abandoning my search for an escape route, and offered a truce smile. My gaze landed on the tattoo on his chest, and the smile died.

I'd seen some of Eddie's tattoos in design form, but I'd never seen this one before. It wasn't one Ahanti had designed since I'd known her, and this was the first time I'd seen Eddie's naked chest close up. The actual inking process made me squeamish, so I always chatted with Terrance in the back or faced my chair away while Ahanti worked. In the past, when Eddie's shirt came off, it signaled that I should turn away.

Now I couldn't turn away. Right over his heart, the pattern formed what looked like a gift box. It was subtle. The design was made in such a way that it reminded me of those Magic Eye puzzles that used to give me a headache from crossing my eyes to see the hidden image.

But I saw it. It couldn't be anything else.

Dear God protect me. Eddie was Ahanti's stalker.

20

*M*y throat felt like I'd swallowed a hornet and it went down stinging.

We hadn't considered Eddie as a possibility for Ahanti's stalker because he hadn't been in the day the picture of Geoff appeared. I hadn't thought to reconsider him now that we knew Terrance sent that photo.

Eddie's name was on my list in the back, and even then, I hadn't put the pieces together. He was just Eddie. Quiet, helpful, always-around Eddie.

Eddie, who got more tattoos than was normal and always wanted touch-ups on tattoos Ahanti thought were still fine.

Eddie, who had access to her apartment and the code to her security system because he'd installed it. Which gave him plenty of time to also install the smoke detector with the hidden camera and microphone. He might have even filched it from work. A lot of security companies now offered systems that allowed owners to covertly monitor their homes while they were at work or on vacation or to make sure the babysitter or nanny wasn't abusing their kids.

I had to get out of here. I had to get to a phone. I'd left mine sitting on the desk next to my list of names because I'd been using it to read my notes about the timing of the stalker's messages.

I sidestepped. "I'd better get back to it. My fiancé will be here to pick me up soon."

It was a lie. Ahanti wouldn't be bringing me back a sub if Mark would be back any minute. Hopefully Eddie'd believe it enough to not try anything. He might not even realize I was on to him after all.

He let me pass.

I headed straight for the back room, keeping my pace casual even though my heart was beating so fast it'd prob-ably soon stop from exhaustion.

The lock on the door clicked behind me.

A zing shot down my neck and the hairs stood up as if I'd really been electrified.

Don't panic, Nikki. It's like how your dogs don't chase a rabbit unless it runs. He might simply be locking the door because Ahanti had it locked.

But my instincts said not. Since she was coming right back, he should have left the door open for her. I had to get to my phone and out the back door.

I broke into a sprint, but a large hand clamped down on my arm and dragged me back. I lost my balance. Eddie hauled me back to my feet.

"I thought you were my friend, too," Eddie said. "You and Terrance. But both of you tried to hurt my relationship with Ahanti. You shouldn't have done that. She's my soul mate."

He was going to kill me like he'd killed Cary and like he'd tried to kill Terrance unless I did something. *Play along,* I'd told Ahanti.

But how did I play along when I was an obstacle in the way of what he wanted rather than the object of his affection?

Playing dumb seemed like the next best option.

"I don't know what you mean. Haven't we been working together to keep Ahanti safe? From Cary, remember? And from Terrance. We helped keep her safe from Terrance. I had people add sensors onto her windows and you..." My voice cracked. I sounded frantic, but I couldn't seem to pull myself together. "You made sure Terrance couldn't harm her again."

His fingers pinched into my arm, sending spirals of pain down to my elbow and up to my shoulder. I bit into my cheek involuntarily, and the coppery taste of blood flooded my mouth.

"You didn't help," Eddie said. "You took out the camera I'd put in to watch over her."

There weren't enough ways in my vocabulary to say

crap to get me through this. I wasn't going to be able to convince him that I was on his side. My next best option was to stall him. Ahanti and Lucas would be back soon. Lucas would know something was wrong as soon as the door was locked and no one answered it.

"I didn't know that camera was yours. I would have left it there so you could keep protecting her if I'd known that. I thought it belonged to Terrance, remember?"

Indecision flickered across Eddie's face, then he pulled me toward the back office. "I'm sorry, Nicole. I liked you. I just can't take the chance. She's finally starting to see that I'm the one she's meant to be with. I can't risk you messing that up. It was bad enough you brought in other people to her apartment. That made me look bad. Like I couldn't take care of her."

"She knows you can take care of her," I said.

It seemed like he'd stopped listening. He didn't even acknowledge me with so much as a glare.

He dragged me past the desks, my cell phone too far out of reach. Even if I could break away and grab it, I'd never have time to dial 911 before he snatched it back. Then he'd smash the phone and my head right along with it.

We were headed for the back door. My best chance seemed to be to wait until we were outside and then scream *fire*. I'd read somewhere once that if you screamed for help in a city, no one would come, but if you screamed that there was a fire, everyone would run in your direction.

I sure hoped this was one of the times the Internet was right.

We reached the door. Eddie spun me around and wrapped his arm around my neck before I could lower my chin to stop him. Panic scurried up into my throat, blocking my air. He'd been so smart in going undetected through all of this. Perhaps he didn't intend to allow me to walk out of here on my own.

"Ahanti will wonder what happened to me," I blurted.

He pressed me back against his bare chest. He smelled like sweat and metal and antiseptic. "I'm going to tell her that you got a call and went outside to take it. How am I supposed to know where you went after that?"

If he gave her that story, she'd think the stalker grabbed me, and she'd never suspect it was Eddie all along. She'd stop his tattoo, he'd go home, and she and Lucas would call the police. By then, Eddie would be well on his way to disposing of my body.

Not that I'd care by that point. I'd be dead and in heaven with my Uncle Stan.

As much as I missed him, I didn't want to have our reunion today.

In some back corner of my mind, I recognized that my brain was running in the crazy circles it sometimes fell into, but pulling it out required more willpower than I seemed to possess at the moment.

Eddie tightened his grip. He leaned his head down slightly. "If you fight me or scream, I'll snap your neck."

The way he said it, I believed him. There was a hardness to his tone that I'd never heard before—one that said he was the kind of man who'd rather commit suicide by cop, getting himself shot, instead of going to prison. He'd have no problem taking me out with him.

That thought alone would have buckled my knees had he not essentially been dragging me out the back door by my neck.

He hauled me into the alleyway behind Skin Canvas.

My advice to play along kept repeating in my head. Dead was dead. If I went with him, I might find another way to escape. He couldn't take me anywhere far right now. If we both disappeared, Ahanti would be suspicious of him, and he knew it.

So he must be intending to put me somewhere for now and come back to kill me later, when he wasn't pressed for time and at risk of someone witnessing my murder.

Eddie turned us down another side street where three cars parked. We went around to the back of the first car, and it beeped like he'd hit a clicker to unlock it. The trunk popped open.

My mouth went dry. I hadn't thought through where he planned to put me. His car made sense in a twisted I've-killed-before-and-I'll-do-it-again way.

Not only were the buildings butting up to the alleyway made of bricks—and therefore fairly sound-resistant—but I wouldn't know whether the owners of the other cars were near enough to hear me if I screamed. Likely they were working in a building along this street and wouldn't be back until the end of the day.

By then it'd be too late. I'd have died from heat stroke in his trunk. He wouldn't have to kill me directly.

The arm linked around my throat tightened again, cutting off my air supply. I instinctively grabbed his arm and tugged at it. He loosened it again, and I gasped in a breath.

I realized too late to do anything about it that he'd used it as a way to distract me while he grabbed something from the trunk.

"Hold out your hands, crossed at the wrists and knuckles together."

For one breath, I considered fighting him, but those few seconds without air had been enough. He was too strong. I wouldn't be able to break free.

I held out my wrists and he locked a zip tie around them. It cut into my skin, and an ache spread down into my hands.

What kind of a man carries zip ties around in his trunk? a hysterical little voice in my head shouted.

But I knew. The kind who wanted Ahanti, believed she belonged to him, and was going to do whatever it took to make that happen. In his delusional world, she loved him. She just didn't realize it yet. He must have planned to take her back to his apartment or somewhere else he'd set up for them and keep her until she realized it.

Today had probably been the planned day. With

Terrance out of the way, he would have expected them to be alone in the studio.

Eddie dropped his grip on my throat and tipped me into the trunk in one move. My head smacked into something solid, and the air rushed from my lungs. Before I could grab a full breath, the trunk slammed shut.

Darkness blocked my eyes, and sweat beaded on my upper lip and forehead. Even though the side street where Eddie had parked was in partial shade, it still had to be well over 100 degrees in the trunk. The air was stuffy, clogging my nose and my throat.

The cautions on TV and the radio about leaving pets and children in a car on a hot day said they had about ten minutes before the temperatures in the car reached 160 degrees or more, even with the windows cracked. I didn't have a window cracked in here.

Think, think, think.

Eddie hit a clicker to unlock and pop his trunk. That meant his car was newish. All cars made after 2001 were supposed to have a safety release in the trunk. My parents had once defended a kidnapper in a case where they argued that the victim should have been able to free herself if she'd wanted to for that very reason.

The safety release was supposed to glow in the dark.

It wasn't anywhere from my waist down.

I wriggled around, but the trunk was tiny. I wasn't quite in the fetal position, but it came close. From the corner of my eye, I spotted the tiny glow back above my head. There was no way I was going to be able to get my hands behind my head to reach the release as long as they were tied together.

I'd give a lot right now to tell my parents how flawed their argument had been. The poor kidnapped woman could have been zip tied like I was or duct taped or tied with a rope.

They'd won that case.

"Focus, Nicole." My voice sounded muffled even to me, like the small space shrunk it somehow.

I strained against the zip ties. Numbness flooded my fingers.

Bad idea. Not only was I not going to be able to break out of them that way, but I might cut off my circulation.

I slithered my hands around, but Eddie had been careful. I was too tightly bound to wriggle a hand loose.

My purse was back in Skin Canvas…or more precisely, probably out in the dumpster behind Skin Canvas, along with my phone by now, since Eddie's story was going to be that I'd left to take a call. If I'd had it, I might have been able to get out my fingernail cutters.

I moved my hands along as much of the trunk as I could. It was smooth to the touch. Nothing remotely sharp enough to cut through plastic. Trying to chew my way through would only break my teeth.

Tears pressed at the back of my throat and clogged my nose even more. This was both the right time for tears and the worst possible time.

Literally the only tool I had was my shoe laces. They seemed like they'd be better to tie something with than to cut something with, but they were nylon, like the leashes Mandy now had a vendetta against.

That might mean my nylon laces would also be abrasive enough to create the friction needed to snap the zip ties.

I squirmed around, bringing my knees up closer into my chest, and reached my fingers as far as they would go. They brushed the edge of a lace.

I strained further, every muscle in my body pleading with me to stop. I pinched one end between my pointer and middle finger and moved along until I had the other lace end trapped in my other hand. When I released the bow, I'd need to have hold of both ends.

The bow gave way.

My tongue felt thick in my mouth, and my shirt was so damp against my body that it felt like it was trying to smother me. The car around me seemed to be moving, swaying, even though I knew it was standing still. I didn't have long before I'd pass out in the heat. I used to think freezing to death was the worst possible way to go. I'd been wrong. At least when I'd been close to hypothermia, I'd felt drowsy, not sick to my stomach and dizzy the way I did now.

Sirens carried faintly from a distance, coming closer. For the first time in my life, I wished telepathy was a real thing. Then I could mentally message the officers to come find me. I was here.

I let out a breath. I couldn't let me mind wander.

I maneuvered one end of the shoelace up until I had it between my teeth. My fingers were so weak and numb I could barely tie the knot.

The driver's door slammed, and I jerked. The lace slid through my fingers. Thankfully, I'd already completed the knot.

Eddie shouldn't have been back, but no one else would be climbing into his car. Had he managed to convince Ahanti to come with him? He could have talked her into letting him drive her home while Lucas waited for the police.

I hadn't heard voices.

Then again, I hadn't heard him coming back at all.

The car engine roared to life.

My fingers trembled. This was bad. Really bad. Once Eddie got out onto the highway, there'd be no way I could jump from the car even if I got the trunk open. I'd be killed on impact, and that was assuming I managed to avoid being run over by the cars and semi-trucks behind him.

And if he had Ahanti with him, no one else would know he took her. He could take her anywhere. Out into the Virginian countryside even. That's likely where he'd be heading to dispose of my body.

I had to get out before he hit the highway. I had to tell the police that Eddie was the guy they were looking for.

I tested the knot. If it let go, I wouldn't get the laces back, not with how close the confines were.

It seemed tight.

My vision spun and tunneled. I breathed in through my nose and out through my mouth, and sawed my feet up and down like I was riding the world's tiniest bicycle.

The zip ties snapped.

Thank you, Lord!

My hands throbbed, but I wedged them over my head. The car was moving now.

My knuckles hit something that seemed out of place. I grabbed it, pulled, and the trunk popped. It bounced up and down with the motion of the car, threatening to crush anything that dared to get between its jaws.

I had no choice. It was either risk being battered by the trunk or face Eddie whenever he reached his destination, assuming I didn't die of heat stroke first.

I braced my hands on the trunk lid and crawled to my knees, then into a squat.

I shoved the trunk and dove.

The pavement came up before I could tuck into a ball. Pain burned through so many parts of my body that it all flamed together into more than I could stand.

The last thing I heard before blacking out was more sirens.

21

The face leaning over me when I opened my eyes wasn't Jesus or my Uncle Stan, so I knew I'd survived.

Oddly enough, it wasn't my mom or Mark either. It wasn't even Ahanti.

It was Geoff.

Which was unfortunate, since the fall seemed to have knocked my filter loose. The first thing out of my mouth was, "I'm getting really tired of hospitals."

Geoff's mouth lengthened in that expression people got when they weren't sure whether what you'd said was meant to be funny or not. "Mark will be back any minute. I sent him to get us some coffee before he paced a hole in the floor."

No mention of Ahanti.

My tongue went numb, making trying to speak like

trying to talk around a mouthful of peanut butter. I hadn't been conscious to tell anyone what I'd figured out. He might have grabbed her. She might have been in his car. Or he might be after her right now.

"It was Eddie." I tried to sit up, and pain burned down my left arm and leg, stealing my breath. "You have to warn Ahanti and tell the detective."

Geoff reached out both hands toward me and patted the air, like he was afraid to touch me for fear of hurting me but also afraid to let me keep flopping around like a suffocating fish. "We know. It's okay. Ahanti's with your mom, giving a statement to the police right now. She'll be here as soon as she's done."

Giving a statement to the police? That meant I couldn't have been unconscious long, but it seemed like I'd missed a lot regardless.

Mark came through the door with a cup of coffee in each hand. The relief that erased the lines in his face as soon as his gaze met mine worked better than whatever pain killer the hospital had me on.

"I'm sorry this wasn't the vacation we planned," I said.

Which was probably the last thing I needed to be thinking about at the moment, but everything still seemed to be garbled up in my head.

Mark handed Geoff one of the cups, and Geoff gave him the chair next to me.

"How are you feeling?" he asked.

Half of me felt okay, but the other half felt like I'd been

run down by a car rather than diving out of one. I didn't want to know what was wrong with me until I found out what had happened, though. I was still breathing, so everything else would heal.

"Why is Ahanti giving a statement to Detective DeGoey? What happened?"

"The detective wants to talk to you to ask that very thing when he finishes with Ahanti." Mark took my hand more gently than usual. "All we know is that you jumped from a moving car. A woman saw it happening when she was walking back to where she'd parked, and she called it in."

If they didn't know anything about what went on, that meant Eddie wasn't talking. Or that they hadn't caught him yet. "If you don't know what happened, how did you know Eddie was Ahanti's stalker?"

It was too bad Ahanti wasn't here to see Geoff's grin. It was the same one he got when she showed him an art-gallery worthy design. Terrance was wrong when he said Geoff wasn't a good match for Ahanti because he didn't want a tattoo of his own. He was a better match because he didn't and yet he loved her for what she did despite not fully understanding it.

"Ahanti figured it out," he said. "She was ordering the subs and realized that Eddie's handwriting was close to the handwriting of her stalker. She called Detective DeGoey right away. He sent the police to Skin Canvas."

That explained the sirens I'd heard. It also explained

why Eddie came back to his car sooner than I expected. He must have figured out the sirens were for him. Maybe he thought someone saw him dump me in the trunk or that I'd managed to send a message for help before he grabbed me.

I told them what happened after Ahanti and Lucas left. "Have the police captured Eddie yet?"

Mark's face went the color of spoiled milk. The expression on his face sent a shiver down into my core.

Mark set aside his coffee cup and cradled my hand in both of his. "Eddie tried to evade the police and lost control of his car. It flipped at least three times and hit a concrete barricade roof-first. He didn't make it."

Mark's expression finally made sense. If I'd still been in the trunk, I'd be dead, too. The thought didn't quite sink in, but I knew from experience that it eventually would. It'd become another thing that I had to work through with my therapist and my PTSD support group.

For now, I'd accept the numbness gratefully. "So how bad am I hurt?"

Mark smiled just enough for his dimples to peek out. "Not as bad as it could have been. You lost a layer of skin on your arm and thigh, and the doctor thinks you have a bone bruise on your knee. You'll be on crutches for a few weeks, and you might need some physio, but…"

But given how bad it could have been, physio and crutches were a small price to pay.

There was one thing about it all that still worried me

though. "Does this mean we're going to have to miss our flight?"

~

WE DID END UP HAVING TO DELAY OUR RETURN HOME. SINCE we didn't have travel insurance, the airline refused to refund our money or change our flights until we let my dad talk to them. Even airline bigwigs were no match for him.

The extra couple of days in DC turned out to be a benefit. After everything that happened, Ahanti and Geoff eloped after all. Ahanti decided that a big wedding wasn't as important as being married to Geoff, and Geoff decided that leaving most of his stuff in storage until they could find a bigger place was a small sacrifice to make to be with Ahanti.

And Terrance was even well enough to attend, albeit in a wheelchair. Mark and I picked him up for the ceremony, which also gave me my chance to apologize.

Terrance, back to his old self, barely seemed to pay attention to it.

He and Ahanti had already had a long talk as soon as he was allowed visitors. Ahanti agreed to give him another chance, but she wouldn't be loaning him any more money. If Terrance so much as asked, he'd be finding himself a new place to work.

Because my crutches made returning the rental car and

then catching a shuttle to Dulles almost impossible, my dad actually offered to drive us.

Mark went inside to get a wheelchair for me, leaving my dad and me alone for the first time since I'd moved to Fair Haven.

My dad had never been a man who tolerated small talk, and I knew better than to ask if he and Mom would be up to Fair Haven before the wedding. My mom had already taken too much time off to visit in May, and my dad got twitchy with the day or two he'd taken off for our truncated sailing expedition. They'd be there for the wedding, but not much more.

I still didn't know where our relationship stood. My engagement to Mark seemed to have mellowed him enough that he was talking to me again at least, but things still weren't the way I wanted them to be.

I'd been brave enough to talk to my mom, and it'd made things better between us than they'd ever been before. Things with my dad couldn't get much worse, so I really didn't have anything to lose.

"If Mark and I decide not to move to DC, will we go back to you giving me the silent treatment? It's not going to affect my decision. I'd just like to know what to expect."

It came out a lot more confrontationally than I'd intended. I cringed internally, but kept my body perfectly still.

But my dad actually smiled. And it almost looked proud.

It was like I was Dorothy in the old *Wizard of Oz* movie. I stepped out of the black and white and into technicolor and saw things the way they truly were for the first time.

My dad had been angry because he saw me as weak and foolish. In standing up to him during this visit, I'd finally earned the respect that I could never get by trying to do everything his way or by avoiding a confrontation with him. Those things had only reinforced his opinion of me as someone who couldn't think for herself enough to be trusted to make good decisions.

He reached down beside his seat and handed me a manila envelope. "This should help you along toward making the right decision."

He jutted his chin toward the envelope in the universal sign for *go ahead*.

I pulled open the flap. Inside was an official offer for a job, written up in the same way that my parents would present it to any new prospective employee. Only this time, it was for me. When I'd graduated and passed the bar, there'd never been an official offer. It was assumed I'd work for my parents, and that's what I did. I didn't look for other jobs. I never considered negotiating over what my dad stated they'd pay me.

This offer made my previous salary look paltry. Mark and I would easily be able to afford a house with a yard for the dogs if I accepted. It also included the promise of a partnership after two years—a carrot making it more palatable for me to return to being a defense attorney.

Once I was a partner, I'd have more control over what cases I worked on and the role I played in them.

My dad tapped a finger on the edge of the papers. "Your mother also insisted I include the person you should contact if you'd rather work longer hours for less money."

His tone of voice let me know clearly what he thought about that idea, but he kept it to himself otherwise.

I flipped to the last page. My mom had written down a name, phone number, and short message. *Assistant DA is moving to another state in six months. They'll be looking to replace him.*

I tucked the papers back into the envelope and threw my arms around my dad. I didn't care that hugging wasn't what we did.

Because I finally saw those offers for what they were. They weren't my parents trying to control me. They're weren't my parents meddling.

They were my parents saying, in the only way they could, that they loved me and wanted me to come back home. Now the challenge was that Mark and I needed to decide if we wanted to stay in Fair Haven or return to DC.

BONUS RECIPE: TRAVELER'S MAPLE SYRUP CHEESECAKE

INGREDIENTS:

½ cup unsalted butter

3½ cups graham cracker crumbs (this makes a thick crust, so you can use less if you like a thinner crust)

1½ cups maple syrup, plus some for drizzling

32 ounces of cream cheese

4 large eggs

1 tablespoon vanilla extract

½ cup whipping cream

TOOLS:

2 large bowls

1 small microwave-safe bowl

10-inch springform pan

aluminum foil

electric mixer

whatever utensils you like for stirring

INSTRUCTIONS:

1. Preheat oven to 350 degrees F.
2. Melt butter in the microwave. A great tip to keep your butter from burning or turning grainy is to heat it until only about half the butter is melted. Take it out and stir. The heat from the melted butter will melt the rest.
3. In a large bowl, mix together the melted butter, graham cracker crumbs, and a half cup of the maple syrup.
4. Press crumb mixture into the bottom and up the sides of your springform pan. Wrap a layer or two of aluminum foil around the pan. (It helps keep the cheesecake filling from leaking out while it's cooking.)
5. In another large bowl, beat the cream cheese until smooth, scraping down the sides of the bowl as necessary. Add the maple syrup and beat again until combined.
6. Add the eggs one at a time. Beat well after each egg.
7. Add vanilla and whipping cream and beat a final time until they're just combined.

8. Pour the filling into the pan. Bake on the middle rack of the oven for around an hour.
   (Cheesecake should be set on the edges and a little jiggly in the center.)
9. Cool the cheesecake completely in the pan on a cooling rack.
10. Cover the top of the cheesecake with a layer of plastic wrap and chill for at least 8 hours. Two days is better.
11. To serve, remove the side of the pan, cut into wedges, and drizzle each wedge with maple syrup.

SERVES: 8

Travel Tip: If you want to bring this cheesecake with you on a long-distance trip, transfer it to a cardboard round after it's completely chilled, then wrap it in three layers— parchment paper, then plastic wrap, and finally aluminum foil. Freeze it completely and package it in a tight box. Carry it on the plane with you and store it under your seat. (This only works if you make the full-fat version above. Don't freeze the lightened version because the light cream cheese doesn't survive the freezer well.)

Tip for a Lighter Version: If you're trying to watch your weight because you happen to have a fancy dress you'll need to fit in soon (or simply because you want to be able to zip up your pants), you can make a couple changes to the recipe. Use light cream cheese, swap half the eggs for egg replacement, and use buttermilk instead of whipping cream. You can also cut the recipe in half for a smaller cheesecake and bake it in a 7-inch springform pan instead.

LETTER FROM THE AUTHOR

I hope you enjoyed seeing Nicole go back to Washington, DC. I thought it'd be fun to take Nicole and Mark to the big city for a change.

In the next book, they'll be back to Fair Haven, but all still isn't well. They'll be planning their wedding and trying to decide whether to make their home in Fair Haven or in DC. And a face from Elise's past is back and causing trouble. Nicole will find herself defending a man that she isn't sure is innocent.

If you'd like to know as soon as Book 7 (*Tapped Out*) releases, sign up for my newsletter at www.smarturl.it/emilyjames.

If you liked *Capital Obsession*, I'd also really appreciate it if you also took a minute to write a quick review. Reviews help me sell more books (which allows me to keep writing them), and they also help fellow readers know if this is a book they might enjoy.

Love,

Emily

ABOUT THE AUTHOR

Emily James grew up watching TV shows like *Matlock*, *Monk*, and *Murder She Wrote*. (It's pure coincidence that they all begin with an M.) It was no surprise to anyone when she turned into a mystery writer.

She loves cats, dogs, and coffee. Lots and lots of coffee…lots and lots of cats, too. Seriously, there's hardly room in the bed for her husband. While they only have one dog, she's a Great Dane, so she should count as at least two.

If you'd like to know as soon as Emily's next mystery releases, please join her newsletter list at www.smarturl.it/emilyjames.

She also loves hearing from readers.

www.authoremilyjames.com
authoremilyjames@gmail.com

Made in the USA
Lexington, KY
08 August 2017